Christmas on ICE

Palmer City VOLTAGE

BOOK 2

KERRY EVELYN

Swan Press

Christmas on Ice by Kerry Evelyn © 2021

Edited by SharpEditor

Proofed by BookNookNuts

Cover design and interior formatting by Chris Kridler, Sky Diary
Productions

Paperback ISBN: 979-8-9851254-3-6

Printed in the United States of America

First Printing: November 2021 Swan Press

To my Cabochon Girls!
What a gift you are!

TRASK

*C*old. The biting October wind cut into the heated cab of my new full-size pickup as I opened the door in the lot of Brewski's Sports Pub & Grille in Palmer City, Colorado. I was grateful for the upgrade—especially its dependable heater—since the harsh winter was about to set in. With my new two-way contract with Denver's NHL team, I'd be able to make the monthly payments without an issue and still send money home to my parents for Mama's medical bills.

I pulled my knit hat low over my forehead and tucked my chin into the collar of my parka. Back home in Charleston, it was just starting to cool off, and I missed the warmth of the lazy fall nights and the salty scent of the ocean along the Battery.

Tonight, the team should be celebrating a win, but we'd come up short again. We'd lost two of our best players to the new expansion team, and the lines hadn't fully adjusted to the changes. My former defensive partner and I had been able to read each other's minds, and I hadn't found that kind of chemistry with any of the other defensemen yet.

I scanned the lot for familiar cars and wasn't surprised to see only a few players had shown up. I fell into step beside my roommate and our team captain, goalie Jason Dexter, who'd pulled in just ahead of me.

"Sorry about that last goal, man," I shouted into the wind. "We left you exposed."

"I should have blocked it. Rainoni knows my weakness is above my right shoulder. I should've expected that's where he'd aim."

"Still." I stepped around him to open the door, and we entered the warm restaurant. "Trotter was in the wrong place, and I couldn't get to you fast enough."

"We'll get 'em next time." Jason shrugged and pulled his hood off. "I see Lauren." He nodded to a table beside the brewing equipment that lined the left wall. "Looks like she brought one of her teacher friends for you." He grinned, and I shook my head. Jason's girlfriend had tried to play cupid when I moved in with him, but unlike him, she'd given up when she realized I wasn't interested in any of the women she worked with.

There was only one person here I really wanted to see, and a quick search of the restaurant came up empty.

Jason reached the table first and bent to give Lauren a kiss. I draped my coat over the back of the chair next to Lauren's friend as the two women gathered up and stacked the papers that were strewn all over the table.

"I'm Trask." I offered my hand to the woman next to me. "Do you and Lauren work together?"

"Alicia. Sort of. I'm her intern this semester." The petite

blonde smiled shyly as we shook. "Do you play for the Voltage, too?"

"I do." I sat and turned to Lauren. "A grade change and an intern this year? That's awesome."

Lauren smiled. "It's a gift, really. Without Alicia, I'd never get all these essays graded. It's bad enough I had to miss the game for a staff meeting."

"You didn't miss much," I grumbled, trying to look past her to the bar area.

Lauren caught my eyes wandering. "She's in the snug with Ryleigh."

I groaned. "Am I that obvious?" Next to the bar, the small room, called a snug, had a booth and table inside. Its door was closed, but its side window faced the bar and was a perfect corral for the three-year-old daughter of our favorite server.

As if my thoughts could conjure her, Kami Spencer opened the door and exited the snuggery. A flash of lime green raced past her and straight for our table. I put my arm out to steady the little girl as she tripped on her fairy costume and came to an unbalanced stop next to us.

"Mr. Tiggerman! Did you win?" The brown curls piled on her head bounced as she spoke.

Jason snorted, and I shot him a dirty look. The team had nicknamed me Tiger, since that was my college mascot. Ryleigh had heard one of them call me that and declared, as only a three-year-old could, that she'd call me Tigger because he was fluffy and not scary and I wasn't scary either.

I hadn't had the nerve to ask why she thought I was fluffy.

"Not tonight, Ry." I bent down to be eye level with her. "What are you doing up so late?" I glanced at her mother, who handed me a menu.

"Daddy had to work, so he brought me here. And Mommy has to work, so I get to watch Thinter Bale and Peetah Pahn in the little room!"

"Oh yeah? 'Peetah Pahn'? Not Peter Pan?" I met Kami's eyes, and she shrugged, tucking a loose strand of brown hair from her ponytail behind her ear. The casual gesture belied the worry in her eyes. Her ex-husband had been leaving Ryleigh here more and more often lately.

Ryleigh scoffed. "Wendy says Pee-*tah Pahn*, so that's how *I* say it."

"Well, that makes sense. Sounds like fun."

"It is! But Mommy said I have to go soon." She pouted. "Auntie Brenna is coming to take me home and put me to bed."

Brenna Brewer, the restaurant owners' daughter, was good friends with Kami, and I'd learned they'd been roommates in college.

"That's probably a good idea." I leaned close to her. "I heard fairies need a lot of sleep to make their magic work."

"Oh, they do." She nodded. Ryleigh motioned with her hand for me to bend down close to her. She cupped her hands around my ear. "Daddy says Mommy is a worry worm."

"Do you mean worry wart?" I whispered. She stepped back with disdain on her face. "No, warts are GROSS. Worms are cute. Like Mommy. Don't you think so?" Ryleigh caught my gaze and held on. This girl was fierce.

"I absolutely think so."

She giggled, and I became aware of the three sets of eyes staring at us. I cleared my throat and straightened.

Kami must have noticed, too. "Ryleigh, sweetie, go on back

to your movie so I can get Mr. Jason and Mr. Trask's orders, okay?"

Ryleigh sighed dramatically. "Oooookaaaay." I watched her go, a smile playing at my lips. She reminded me of my niece back home.

I looked up at Kami, searching her eyes and hating the pain I saw there. "Are you okay?" I asked softly.

She nodded. "What can I get y'all?"

"Oooh, I love your accent," Alicia said. I'd forgotten she was there. "Where are you from?"

"South Carolina," Kami said.

"So's Trask," Jason offered.

"That's right!" Kami's expression lightened. "How are you liking the weather? Took me a good three years to get used to it."

I grinned. "I'm definitely not used to it yet. But I'm looking forward to trying my hand at snow tubing this year. Skiing is definitely not my thing."

She laughed. "Same." Kami glanced back to the television screen behind her. "Big storm coming in tonight. Quinn's closing the kitchen at eleven. Do y'all know what you want?"

We gave her our orders and fell into easy conversation. I watched Brenna come in and take Ryleigh, and we closed out our checks around eleven so Kami could get home to Ryleigh. By the time we got going, though, it was almost midnight, and a glance out the window confirmed the snow had begun to fall.

"Snow day tomorrow?" I asked Lauren as we put on our coats.

"No doubt. More time to grade these essays." She grimaced. "Be careful out there, Trask. I know you were here last winter and your new truck is designed to handle whatever Colorado can throw at it, but still, be cautious, okay?"

"Don't worry about me." I grinned. "I plan to enjoy the alone time while he's at your place."

I said goodbye and headed to my car. The snow was already coming down steadily.

The engine roared to life. "Yeah, baby," I said. Nothing like the groaning old pickup I'd driven here from South Carolina when I'd signed with the team. I let it warm up for a few minutes and slowly pulled out of the lot, my tires crunching over the blanket of snow that had already accumulated.

The thick flakes made it difficult to see. I tensed up as I held the wheel tightly. I'd driven in worse, but it was dark, and black ice could be hiding anywhere.

Not far down the road, I saw the blinking hazard lights of a small car on the shoulder. I pulled to a stop behind it and left the truck running as I battled the icy sting of the falling snow. The car was covered in about an inch of powder. I hoped whoever was inside had help on the way.

I used my glove to brush away the snow on the driver's side window and jumped when I saw the face of the woman in the car. Equally startled, Kami Spencer stared back at me with an open mouth and wide eyes.

2

KAMI

*H*ow embarrassing. This was the last place I ever imagined being alone with Trask Emerson.

After my initial shock, I realized he was trying to ask if I was okay. The side of his gloved hands, cupped in a circle around his perfect mouth, were forming words I couldn't hear over the pulse beating in my head.

"What?!" I shouted. I leaned toward the window to hear him better.

"Are you okay?!"

I formed my hands around my mouth and pressed them to the glass, mimicking his. "Yes!"

"What?! Can you open your window?!"

I shook my head, then realized he probably couldn't see me. I cracked open my door and forced a smile at the hottest guy I'd ever met in real life. "I'm fine!" I shouted. Dang, the wind was loud. And cold. "Window is frozen shut! Dead battery, I think? Roadside assistance is on the way!"

He gently pushed the door shut and talked through the closed window, his warm breath steaming the cold glass. "I can give you a jump, then you can warm up in my truck till your heat gets going again."

If I hadn't already been shaking, I would have shivered at that remark. Trask had that effect on me, and I tried to ignore it. It was better that way. I'd been divorced officially for four months but out of love for years. I tried to avoid Trask as much as possible when he came into the restaurant because I felt zazzled even just in his presence. Not even my ex had ever set off butterflies that fought to break free from my body that way.

I sighed.

"Okay!" I shouted back at him, realizing he was waiting for an answer. I gave him a thumbs-up and twisted in my seat to watch him walk back to his truck, but the darkness and snow were so thick, I lost sight of him after a few feet. A few moments later, his truck was parked facing my car. I popped the hood and opened my door.

"I'll flash my lights when it's time for you to turn the key and rev your engine!!" he shouted.

"Okay!

I scrunched down to watch with fascination through the tiny opening at the bottom of the hood as he attached the jumper cables and jogged back to his truck. I hadn't known until tonight that he was from South Carolina. I'd known he was from the South, and sometimes I caught traces of a faint accent, a familiar dialect that hit me straight in the gut. The sound of *home*.

I'd been in Colorado for almost nine years. I'd come here for college while Sutton attended a state college back home. He'd joined the Air Force, and after we graduated, he received orders to report to the base in Colorado Springs. We'd hastily

—and naively—gotten married so we could live together in base housing. *What a mistake.* Just as we realized how incompatible we were, we got pregnant with Ryleigh. It was around that time I discovered my high school "sweetheart" had never been faithful to me.

All the while, I was working on my master's and doctorate degrees in earth sciences. At this point, I had about another year left on the latter, but if I hustled, I could finish in the spring and walk in May. Once I had it, I'd go back home to play in the marshy Lowcountry muck and raise Ryleigh among family.

He flashed the lights, and I pressed the brake pedal to the floor. *Here we go.* I turned the key and revved the gas, praying as the engine stalled and then roared to life.

After a few minutes, he got out again and appeared at my window. "Passenger door is unlocked. Go on in and warm up!"

He didn't have to tell me twice.

I was out of my car and in his truck in record time. When my frozen backside settled in the seat, I was surprised and moved to learn he'd already set the automatic seat heater to warm up for me.

When I saw him coming, I lifted my scarf to cover my face as Trask opened his driver's side door and climbed up. Even after all the winters in Colorado, the force of the cold chilled me to the bone. I wondered how long it took hockey players to not feel it. Or did they?

I lowered my scarf. "Thanks, Trask." Reaching into the pocket of my coat, I felt for my phone. "Do you think it's good to go? This happened the other day in the restaurant parking lot, and it was fine after a jump. It seemed okay today."

"It might be your alternator. I had to replace the one on my old truck last year."

"Gosh, I hope not." The last thing I wanted to spend my meager savings on was car repairs.

"Let's wait a few minutes and see." He pulled off his gloves and hat and shook out his hair, which was longer in the front and fell over his right eye. He shook his head, flicking his hair to the side.

I wanted to touch it, brush the snowflakes out of his hair—

Instead, I swallowed and pulled up the app for roadside assistance. "The app says they're still about an hour out."

"If it quits, I can take you home," he said. I met his gaze and couldn't pull away.

Or speak.

He cleared his throat. "So ... Where in South Carolina are you from?"

"Summerville. Right outside—"

"Charleston," he drawled with a grin, and I felt myself returning his smile. "That's where I'm from. Right on the South Battery."

"Oh wow. Those homes are beautiful." I'd spent many a day strolling along the Battery, imagining the people who lived in the old homes and wondering what their stories were. It was my favorite area of the city. I'd known he was from Charleston, but a lot of people say they're from the nearest city when they move away from there. To grow up right in the heart of the city must have been amazing.

He shrugged. "Ours has been in the family forever and needs some work. It's expensive to maintain, and with my mom's cancer treatment bills, we've had to put off some of the updates that need to be done."

"I'm sorry to hear that. Is your mom okay?"

He shifted in the seat and stared out the windshield. "Yeah, for now. This is the second time she's had it, so she's more run-down, and the side effects are a lot worse than the first time. Some days she's okay. Some days, she's not. My younger sister Brooklyn works from home, so she's there with her all day while Dad's at work. But she's getting married in December, so I'm not sure what we'll do then."

"That's really tough, Trask. It must be hard for you to be so far away. I miss my family like crazy. I wish I could afford to go back to visit more."

"It's tough, but my new contract will help a bit. And once I get to the NHL ..." He shook his head like he was trying to reset his mind, then flashed another grin. "It wasn't my intention to vent about my family problems. You're just so easy to talk to."

I smiled shyly. "It's okay. I asked, remember?"

His grin widened. "You did. So how about you?"

"Well ..." It was easy to talk to him, too. But how much to tell him? Sutton and I had married way too young, or at least under a lot of pressure. We wanted to be together but weren't ready to make a lifetime commitment. Looking back, it had been doomed before it began. "It's just me and Ryleigh right now, till I finish my doctorate. Her dad and I are divorced after a two-year separation. Our families are in Summerville, and I plan to move back there when I finish my degree."

He nodded. "It's a hard place to leave, isn't it?"

"It wasn't then. But now, with Ryleigh ... I miss my family."

"Do they visit?"

"Not really. They run businesses and can't ever manage to get time off. They're busiest on the weekends." My sisters owned an event-planning business and hosted weddings and parties at our farm. It had been a long time since anyone in my immediate family had been able to visit us.

"That's too bad." Trask's sympathetic expression was warm, but I didn't want him feeling bad for me.

"Do you think it's been long enough?" I asked, gesturing to my car.

"Yeah. Let me clear it off for you." He put his hat and gloves back on and pulled up a brush from the other side of his seat.

"I can help." I opened the door and sucked in a breath at the icy blast. I slid down from the cab and pushed against the wind to get to my car. My long hair whipped in my eyes, blinding me. Opening the door, I felt along the side of the seat to get my own snowbrush before slamming it closed again.

Trask was brushing the snow from the passenger side, so I worked along my side and brushed the snow off the roof first and worked my way down the windows and over to the trunk. We finished at the same time, and while he disconnected the cables, I got in the car, thankful to be back in the warmth.

I cracked open the window, grateful it had unfrozen while the car ran. Amazing what a little heat could do. "Thank you!"

He held up a hand, and I waited for him to appear at my window. "Can I follow you home? My mama would beat me if I didn't make sure you got there okay."

"Sure!" I knew better than to argue with centuries of Southern chivalry. Besides, I liked it. It felt nice to be looked out for. My grandfather had set a standard that Sutton had never lived up to. Somehow I had a feeling Trask came by it naturally, and thinking about it made me feel all swoony inside.

"Don't lose the heat!" *No danger of that. Ha!* He shut the door, and I instantly felt the loss of connection.

"Thanks again!" I waved to him and closed my window, watching him walk back to his truck with a stupid grin on my face.

I didn't have time to be crushing on anyone, but I liked him.

A lot.

And that was a problem.

3

TRASK

I couldn't believe it. We'd finally won a game.

You'd think we'd won a championship or something by the way the fans reacted. I couldn't blame them. My defensive partner, Brendan Trotter, and I had gotten it together and hadn't let many shots get near the goal on our shifts. The other defensive lines weren't as effective, but our forwards had been on fire. We'd won 5-3, and I'd been named one of the three stars of the game.

The wives and girlfriends—Wags as they were known in hockey but collectively called the Pack by our team—had arranged a celebratory late lunch/after-party at Brewski's. We were usually starving after a Sunday afternoon game, but when I arrived at the restaurant, food was the last thing on my mind.

Out of habit, I scanned the interior, looking for Kami. I caught her eye as she exited the function room and waved. She smiled back and hustled to the bar. Behind the bar, Brenna and her brother Drew were filling pitchers with beer and sangria.

I took off my coat and strode into the back room to meet the team.

"Wow, the ladies went all out," I said to Craig Ward, our backup goalie, as I took in the decorations and fanfare in the room.

"When you gonna get a girl, Tiger?" He clapped me on the back. "Svetlana and the rest of the Pack could really use some help with these events and all this—this—decoration stuff."

"You know he has a girl back home, Warden," Brendan said, joining us. "Maybe she'll come to visit?"

I had a girl back home? That was news to me. "What are you talking about, Trotter?"

He shrugged. "Sorry if I outed you, man. Didn't know it was a secret."

"Really, dude, I have no idea what you're talking about. What gave you the idea I had a girlfriend back home?"

"Sure, okay." He grinned. "Saw you video-chatting before the game with your earbuds in. You called her sweetheart, told her you missed her, and blew her kisses. Sounds like a girlfriend to me."

I almost laughed but sipped my drink smugly instead. I'd been talking to my four-year-old niece, Mylee.

I slung my jacket over a nearby chair and helped myself to the buffet. I sensed Kami before I saw her, and once my plate was full, I headed back to my seat to wave her over.

"What can I get you?" she asked. A rosy blush crept up her neck, and I liked knowing that I had the same effect on her that she had on me.

Or she was overheated. She was working hard.

I opted to go with the former hypothesis.

"How's your car?" I asked.

"It was the alternator, just like you suspected."

She sounded cheerful, but I caught a sad undertone. "I'm sorry. That's a pricey fix."

"Nothing I can't handle." Our eyes locked, and I couldn't tear my gaze away. Hers were a deep brown with light flecks that seemed to make them sparkle, even when she seemed troubled.

"Um." Kami broke the spell. "It's okay, really. Last week's tips covered it." She flashed a grin that didn't meet her eyes. "Can I get you a drink? Your usual or water?"

I cleared my throat and straightened up. "The usual. Thanks." Brewski's wasn't just a restaurant; it was an operating brewery with half a dozen unique beers. "And can I try a sample of that new peanut butter one?"

She flashed a grin. "Sure thing. If you like peanut butter, you're gonna love it."

"Sounds great." I watched her go, and when she was out of sight, I realized I'd been oblivious to the silence around me.

"Yeah, Trotter, no decent guy with a girl back home would look at another woman that way," Craig said, elbowing me in the shoulder.

"Huh?" I looked at my teammates to explain.

"You and Kami," Brendan said. "You got it bad, Tiger."

I swallowed and pasted a fake grin on my face. "I don't know what you're talking about. I hardly know her. "

"Seems like you wouldn't be opposed to knowing her better," Craig said. "You can double date with me and Svetlana anytime. Right, Letty?"

His wife wrapped her arm around his waist and raised her eyebrows teasingly. "Sooner than later. I like her. Will be fun."

A date with Kami? The thought swirled in my head. It had been a long time since I'd been on a date, and I had to admit I liked the idea.

4

KAMI

a few days after I got my car back from the auto repair shop, the Voltage gathered at Brewski's again. I stood at the end of the bar, eyes glued to Trask's retreating form as he walked from the bathroom to the function room and disappeared inside. Just the sight of him made my butterflies do loop-de-loops.

My attraction to him had grown gradually since I met him last spring, but especially the last few days. He'd followed me home and flashed his lights, driving on as I pulled into my driveway.

I hadn't been able to stop thinking about him since.

I wondered if he felt a spark. I got the sense he liked me, but for whatever reason, he kept it to himself. Didn't matter, though. I wasn't in a place to start a new relationship, even if I wanted to. I had to think about Ryleigh and our future once I finished my degree. It wouldn't do any good to get attached to a transient professional athlete.

"Kami ..." Brenna's voice cut through my daydream. She and

our friend Chelsea had just come from the game. Chelsea was a member of the Voltage's spirit squad and managed the cheer gym at the Plex, Palmer City's rec complex, where pretty much everything sports- and fitness-related happened. It housed the Voltage's practice rink and a one-stop-shop with restaurants, medical offices, after-school programs, and even Ryleigh's daycare, which many of the athletes' children attended.

My eyes were still fixed on the function room entrance. "Mm?"

I jumped when she poked my shoulder.

"You good?" She smirked with that knowing look of a longtime friend who's on to you.

"Too good, I'm afraid." I placed three pitchers of beer on my tray and sighed. "Wrong time, wrong place, wrong career for a crush."

Chelsea grunted. "Word is he likes you, too. You're single now. Why not see if there's more than vibes between you?"

"You can see *vibes?*" My voice rose with each word, and I had to take a step to keep the tray balanced while they grinned at me like scheming Cheshire cats. They'd been friends since kindergarten and I swear sometimes they shared a brain.

"Oh yeah," Drew interrupted, setting a plate of shepherd's pie bites on the bar between them. "He watches you all the time."

"He—what?"

"Not creepy-like." Drew shrugged. "I bet he wants to ask you out but doesn't know how."

I rolled my eyes. "What is it with guys? It's six words: 'Will you go out with me?' Simple."

"Well …" Drew said, an uneasy tone to his voice. He swallowed. "You're pretty intimidating, Kami."

"Me? Why?" This was news. I was intimidating? To these guys? A professional athlete and restaurant manager? I was a single mom and a student, serving tables to pay for private preschool that was close to work and home so Brenna could help. They were intimidated by *me?* I couldn't believe that.

"Uh …" He looked at Brenna for help.

"Enlighten us, Drew," she said. *Good.* I wanted to know what made me so unapproachable.

He swallowed again. "First, you're super smart. You're getting a doctorate in science. Do you know how many guys had the hots for you when you taught my earth science class last fall?"

I blinked and tried to ignore his last comment. "So? I like to analyze dirt. It's not fancy, I assure you."

Brenna snorted, which caused Chelsea to giggle. I shot them a glare.

Drew continued. "And, well … you have a great kid. But it's a big role to step into for a guy in his twenties." Drew was still an undergrad, so it didn't surprise me he thought that. But Trask was my age, at least according to the Voltage stats.

"She already has a father," I said. Brenna snorted again, and I glared at her. Sutton might not be the most dedicated father, but he wasn't a deadbeat. "I'm not looking for a new dad for Ryleigh. Geez."

I left them at the bar and plastered a smile on my face. The function room was hopping. I greeted the team members I knew. As I set out the third pitcher, my phone vibrated, the sound increasing in urgency by the second.

"Is that your phone?" asked the gentle rolling Russian-accented voice of Kira Antonova, wife of Rurik Antonov, the Voltage's first line right winger. Their daughter, Natasha, was in Ryleigh's preschool class.

"It is. I'll check it in a bit."

"Check now. Might be school. I just got off the phone with the girls' teacher, and they are needing to close early. Food poisoning outbreak."

I gasped. "Are the girls—"

"No, no." She waved her hand. "It was the teachers. Something wrong with a cake they brought in for a staff birthday."

"My ex is on call today," I said. "He should be able to get Ryleigh." But as I spoke, I knew the opposite was true. It was Sutton's day off, but he was likely shacked up with his new girlfriend in her mountain cabin that conveniently—for them —had no cell reception or Wi-Fi.

I tucked the tray under my arm and fished the phone out of my apron pocket. Missed call from the preschool. Another buzz signaled a text.

I scanned the text. "Dammit."

Ms. Spencer, we've been unable to reach Ryleigh's father …

I still had two hours left of my shift, and I could really use the tip from the team to pay for Ryleigh's mini all-star cheer-leading lessons. She'd fallen in love with the sport over the summer, and it wasn't cheap. Child support and loans only went so far.

"I could have our nanny pick her up for you and bring her back here?" Kira asked.

I shook my head as I dialed. "Brenna's not scheduled this afternoon. She just stopped in to help out in case we got swamped. She's Ryleigh's emergency contact. Thank you, though."

"It's no trouble." Kira tossed her long black hair over her shoulder. "We moms can help each other. It's what we do."

"Thank you. I really appreciate it." I'd remember that for next time and add her to Ryleigh's pickup list. I turned to go and spotted Trask leaning against a table on the other side of the room chatting with Brendan Trotter. Brendan lifted his hand, so I made my way over to them.

"Congrats on the game. Can I get you guys anything while you wait for the food?" I looked up and swung my gaze to Trask's perfect face. These two were each six feet four and, from what I'd heard, a veritable wall in front of the net—when they could get in sync. Which they'd done today, earning their first win of the season.

"I'm good," Trask said with a grin and glanced at his friend.

Brendan's neck pinkened ever so slightly. "Can you, uh, give Brenna a message for me?"

I put a hand on my hip. He seemed flustered. This was interesting. "Of course."

"Thanks. I overheard her talking to Drew about clearing a barn? I think it's the one out back? I can help with that. Probably some of the team, too." He looked to Trask for confirmation.

"Sure," Trask said. "It'll go a lot quicker with more of us. We can probably round up a bunch of space heaters, too."

"I can do that," I said. "Anything else?"

"Nah, that's it."

I pulled my gaze from Trask and headed back to the bar. Brenna was on the phone, likely with the school, so I waited until she hung up.

"The preschool—"

"I know. Kira just filled me in. They couldn't reach Sutton."

"Ugh. Well, his loss is my gain. Unless you want me to cover for you here?"

"No, I need to finish my shift. Thanks, Bren. I owe you."

"Someday you can watch my kids. I only hope they're as great as Ryleigh." She grinned.

I filled her in on Brendan's offer. Her reaction was just as curious as his. There had to be something more here. I shrugged it off and went into the kitchen to see if the food for the team was ready.

TWO AND A HALF HOURS LATER, I WAS FINALLY ON MY WAY home. It was early evening but already dark outside, and it took my car longer than usual to heat up. I was grateful for the automatic starter my dad had installed before Sutton and I moved here. I didn't mind the cold—much—unless I was in it for too long.

Palmer City was segmented by Snowpack Creek. Brewski's and the arena were on the east side of town with the original downtown area. The sportsplex where the Voltage practiced and where Ryleigh had her preschool and cheer lessons were on the west side with the newer developments. When Sutton and I separated, Ryleigh and I moved off base and into a small rental home at the southern edge of the downtown area. We were within walking distance of the shops and a playground and not too far from Brewski's, the university, and the Air Force base where her father still lived.

After the recent snowstorm, we'd had a bit of a heat wave —temperatures had reached the low fifties during the day before freezing up again at night. Main Street was especially slick, and the bridge passages over the creek were borderline hazardous.

My light turned green at the Old Town bridge, and as I started to turn left, a large truck ran the light coming from the bridge on my right. I jerked my wheel, swerving to avoid him. As the truck turned south, I struggled to get my front end under control. The car shuddered as I yanked at the wheel and entered the intersection, shaking as I turned onto Cross Creek Trail.

Just another minute to home. Almost there.

Then my wheels hit a patch of black ice.

I leaned back into my seat as I slid, trying to keep calm as my adrenaline spiked. My heart pounded like a deafening drum in my ears, and the onset of panic stole my breath. I wrestled with the steering wheel and coaxed the pedal, but it was no use. The world spun around me as my car continued its forward motion down the empty stretch of road.

A vision of Ryleigh flashed before me, and the fear of not being there for her chilled me to the core. Ryleigh's laughter rang out as the car swung towards the side of the road in slow motion.

I gripped the wheel as tight as I could with shaking hands.

No no no no no!

A thud jarred my whole body and my seat belt snapped against me before everything went dark.

5

TRASK

"Kami? Kami, can you hear me?"

Panic gripped my gut as I tried to jimmy open the driver's-side door of her car. I'd found it facing the wrong direction on the side of the road, the front end stuck in the drainage ditch that paralleled the road. Kami's head lay on the steering wheel, and she wasn't moving.

"Kami!" Her head moved slowly, turning toward the sound of my voice. She blinked a few times and closed them again.

I'd just left the restroom at Brewski's and was on my way out when I overheard Drew on the phone with Brenna. I caught bits of their conversation, enough to know that Kami hadn't made it home. They were sure she was fine, probably just making a quick stop on her way, but Brenna was concerned because she always texted details if she was going to be later than expected.

I'd felt a chill and offered to drive the route and see, just in case.

My feeling proved right. I found her car and jumped into action, leaving my headlights on and pointed at her vehicle. I was about to dial 9-1-1 when she sat back and held up her hand. "I'm fine." Though faint, her voice was clear. She unlocked the door, and I pulled it open. I flexed and unflexed my fingers, unsure if I should touch her or not.

"Are you … okay?" My words wavered, and I swallowed. She placed a hand on her forehead and closed her eyes again. The airbags hadn't deployed, and I worried she might have a concussion. "Did you bump your head? Let me look in your eyes?"

She winced as I turned on my phone's light and pointed it away from her. I gently pried her hand off her forehead. "We have to stop meeting like this," I joked, then cringed. Not the best time for my awkward attempt to try to lighten the situation.

Her lips twitched. "I owe you two now," she whispered.

"You don't owe me anything, Kami." I focused on her pupils. "Pretty sure you have a concussion. I can drive you to—"

"No." Her reply was firm and decisive, in that mom voice my own mother had perfected.

"But—" I started to argue.

"Please. I just want to go home."

I nodded. "Okay. But I'm worried about you."

"I'm just tired. I can walk from here and call the tow company when I get home."

"No need. I can take you home, and the guys and I can pull your car up."

Her sigh of relief sent a wave of warmth through my freezing body. It couldn't be much above zero. The interior of her car wasn't as cold as the outside yet. I hated to think of what could've happened if I hadn't found her when I did.

I sent a group text to the team, asking if anyone could come to help me. I had chains in my truck, but I hadn't yet taken the time to learn how to use them properly.

"Do you have a bag or anything?" I asked. She passed me a tote bag, and I slung it over my left shoulder and then extended my hand to her. "I got you."

I gripped her mittened hand in mine and reached around her to support her back. I was looking for any signs of a neck injury. Sometimes you couldn't feel a pinched nerve or whiplash until you started to move.

She seemed okay, so I pulled her to a standing position. The night was cold but clear, without a wind. Still, I slid my arm around her waist to help guide her up the shallow embankment. She stumbled a little.

"Are you sure you don't want to get checked out?" I loosened my hold as we reached the passenger side of my truck, and I opened the door.

"I'm fine. I got this." She climbed up and settled in the seat. I closed the door and jogged back to her car to survey the scene. There wasn't any visible damage, so I locked it up and shot off another text stating I was bringing her home and would be right back.

I called Brenna as I walked back to my truck. "I've got her. She slid off the road. I think she has a concussion. I'm bringing her home now."

"Yikes. I'm so glad you found her." Brenna breathed a sigh of relief. "Did you call a tow?"

"Nah. The guys and I are going to pull it up."

"Okay. Um … I hate to ask, but Drew has a date tonight. I said I'd close up for him. Do you think you could hang out with Kami and Ryleigh until I can get back to stay with her? I don't think she should be left alone if there's a chance she has a concussion. It'll be pretty late, but definitely before the snow starts. I can't believe we're getting hit again with another big storm!"

"Yeah, no problem." That was a no-brainer. "We'll be right there."

Back at my truck, I climbed in and eased out onto the road. Driving extra cautiously, I drove around the next corner to her small cottage-style home nestled among trees. Trimmed with twinkle lights, it looked like something out of a storybook.

"Cute place," I said, turning into the driveway. "I like the lights."

"Thanks. I know it's only October, but never too early for Christmas lights, right?"

"Nah. I love Christmas. Even here, with all the snow." I smiled at her.

"Yeah. It's magical, isn't it? Like being lost in Narnia." The wistful note to her voice made me want to ask more. I wanted to know everything about her.

"Even got a lamppost. So how did you find this place?" Not a very thought-provoking question, but I wanted to keep her talking and I was curious.

She shifted, and shadows danced across her face. "When we left Sutton—he's my ex—I found the house through the vacation rental place on Main Street. It was only going to be temporary until I found an apartment. But then the owner died, and his daughter didn't know what to do with it. She said we could stay here as long as we want as long as we take care of the property. She was a single mom, too, and gave me a more than fair deal."

"That's awesome. I think it's perfect for you and Ryleigh." I could picture the sweet three-year-old in one of her princess dresses skipping through the woods and throwing rocks in the little pond behind the house. I wondered if there were fish in it and if she'd ever been fishing.

"It really is." She pulled at the door handle, and I was out my door and around to hers faster than a hot knife through butter.

"Let me help?" She nodded and placed her hand in mine.

"Thanks. I can walk on my own, though." I stepped aside and followed her up the brick walkway, lit every few feet by tiny staked lanterns.

The door opened as Kami reached the stoop. Brenna was backlit by the warm glow of the interior lighting and visibly upset. She raised her index finger to her mouth.

"Ryleigh's asleep on your bed," she said to Kami and stepped back to let her inside. "I didn't want to risk waking her if I moved her. She fell asleep watching the fairies."

I stayed on the stoop but peeked inside. Across the room and three steps up, the little princess was sleeping on a daybed in a windowed alcove. My gut tightened. She reminded me so much of my niece, Mylee. But … different. Mylee was well taken care of; my brother-in-law was one of the best guys I'd ever known, and my sister Marsha was a supermom. Kami was, too, but from what I'd seen of her ex, he wasn't a candidate for Dad of the Year.

"She's fine, Bren," Kami assured her, then handed me the keys to her car.

Brenna turned to me. "Go do what you need to do. I'll get her settled while you're gone. When you get back with her car, I'll head out. And thanks for the rescue."

"It's no trouble." I hesitated, but Brenna shooed me away.

After leaving Kami with Brenna, I hurried back to her car. By the time I got there, Jason, Brendan, Rurik, and Noel, our rookie, were already working to pull out the car, shouting commands at each other and grunting.

"What can I do?" I asked Jason. He and Rurik were dragging chains from his truck to Kami's car. I winced, remembering my set of chains in my truck—which I'd left at her place.

"Give Noel the keys so he can steer. You can help Trotter push at the hood. Rury will direct us."

"Got it." I made my way down the slope and tossed Kami's keys to Noel. "Thanks for coming," I said to Brendan.

"Anytime. I was just sitting at the bar nursing a beer I didn't really want, anyway."

"Pull!" Rurik yelled. Brendan and I positioned ourselves at the hood and pushed at the car.

"Then why didn't you leave?" I asked, breathing hard.

He shrugged. "Thought I'd catch Brenna when she got back to chat about her barn!" he shouted back once he'd caught his breath. "Drew said she's going to remodel it into a wedding venue."

"Pull!" Rurik yelled, interrupting my follow-up question. Brendan sure did seem fixated on helping Brenna with that barn. Seemed like I wasn't the only one with a crush.

We grunted as our second attempt lifted the front end of the car onto the road. Noel turned the wheel so that it was parallel to the shoulder, and once the car was in the road, he slid out and jogged over to me with the keys.

"I hope she's okay." The eighteen-year-old was only a few

months out of high school. We were all doing our best to help him adjust to his first time away from home.

"I'll update you all when I get back there. Thanks a lot for coming out."

Rurik snorted. "You sound like you are saying goodbye after a party."

Jason laughed. "It's a Southern thing."

We looked at each other and shrugged. Jay was from Atlanta, and when I'd moved in with him, we'd discovered we had a lot in common, including fiery grandmothers and an obsession with everything fried.

I climbed into Kami's car and adjusted the seat, setting it as far back as it could go. As I drove the short distance to her house, I wondered how she felt about me coming over to babysit.

6

KAMI

"*I* don't need a babysitter, Brenna!" I whined from the end of the couch for probably the dozenth time since Trask brought me home. I rubbed at my eyes and pulled the blanket tighter around me.

She'd insisted on calling the paramedics to have me checked out. I'd consented, but only if she told them no lights or sirens. I didn't want to freak out any of the neighbors—or wake up Ryleigh.

My head was throbbing, and all I wanted to do was go to bed. By the grace of God, Ryleigh had crashed early, but she was on my bed by the full window. The one time I left her there and slept in her bed, she woke up terrified, thinking she was outside in the dark.

"Don't you argue with me, Kamryn Marie Ellis Spencer!" I winced at my full name, and her expression softened. "Please? You heard the recommendation. Someone should stay with you overnight, just in case. What if you pass out and Ryleigh finds you?" I sighed, and she took that as a concession. "I'll come back after I close up. You like Trask. He's just going to sit on your couch and check on you every hour or so."

"I can call Chelsea. I'm sure she—"

"No. She and Jackson are doing their wedding cake tasting tonight, remember?"

I shook my head and stopped when I realized it hurt. "Fine. But I don't have to like it."

"What's not to like? Have you *seen* the guy?" A flush of heat rushed to my cheeks as an image of his kind eyes and teasing grin rushed through my mind, no doubt answering for me. Brenna laughed. "Yeah, I thought so. I'll be back. Get some rest."

She opened the door and jumped back. "Hey, you!" She laughed. Trask stood on the stoop, fist in the air as if poised to knock. "That didn't take long."

Trask handed her the keys to my car, which she dropped into the bowl on the cubby unit by the door. "Yeah, wasn't any trouble. I think they enjoyed it, actually." He only lifted the corner of his mouth, coaxing a tiny crinkle in his cheek, but I couldn't take my eyes off him.

"Guys are so weird." Brenna pulled on her coat and looked back at me.

I mustered a smile. "I'll be fine. Go!" I whispered, with a glance toward Ryleigh. "Just get back here before the storm."

"If it's slow, I'll close up early, promise."

She hurried out, but Trask didn't move. His eyes darted around the space, and his interested expression told me he liked what he saw. I loved our little place. I hadn't had to buy any furniture, and there was room for what little I'd taken from the house on base. I'd let Sutton keep pretty much everything. It gave me peace of mind knowing when Ryleigh was over there that he had everything she needed.

"You can hang your coat on a hook by the door." Slowly, he peeled off his parka, stuffing his hat and gloves into the pockets. Finger-combing his blond waves, he seemed uncertain, so I patted the cushion next to me. "Thanks for your help tonight."

He sank down at the other end of the couch and faced me. His large frame took up half the couch. Despite him just coming in from the cold, I could feel the heat emanating from him. "Anytime, Kami. I'm glad I was there when Brenna called, worried about you."

"Me, too." I glanced over at Ryleigh and suddenly got choked up, realizing what could have happened. "I'm really glad she wasn't with me."

"Yeah." He rubbed the back of his neck. "You want me to carry her to bed for you?"

"Umm." I sighed. "She usually wakes up when she's moved."

"Then I'll tell her she's just dreaming and to close her eyes." He flashed a smile. I quickly looked down at my hands so he couldn't see the effect that smile had on me. "I have a niece her age. I think I mastered the car-seat-to-the-crib while I was home over the summer. Let me try?"

I shrugged and fought a smile. It hurt my face to smile. "Go for it. But if she wakes up …"

"I got her."

He made a show of tiptoeing to the daybed, and I stifled a giggle. He winked as he slipped an arm under Ryleigh's princess-nightgown-clad form and another under her knees.

"Tig-man," she mumbled. "Late to…tea party."

"Shhh," he coaxed. "Close your eyes. Mr. Tiggerman is at your tea party now."

"Be … careful, Tig-man. Pretty teacup. Don't … drop."

"Never," he whispered. "I'll be extra careful." My heart melted right there on the spot.

"Good. 'Cause I'm really pretty."

I covered my mouth as he chuckled. Ryleigh sometimes talked in her sleep, but this was hysterical.

"Yes, you are, baby girl. And don't you worry. I always hold what's in my arms real tight." Our eyes met after he said those words, and I sucked in a breath. I looked away, quickly, but I hadn't wanted to break the hold they'd had on me.

Whoa.

7

TRASK

J set Ryleigh on her bed and pulled the covers up over her. The floorboard creaked behind me, and I turned to find Kami in the doorway.

"Thank you," she whispered. I nodded and turned to leave. She stepped aside as I exited the room and closed the door behind her.

"My pleasure." It really was. Sleeping kids always tugged at my heartstrings. But I wasn't thinking about Ryleigh anymore.

We were still standing outside Ryleigh's room. I couldn't think of anything to say, and she wasn't talking either. But the way we were looking at each other ... I was starting to feel warm all over.

I held up my hand. "Follow my finger?" I needed some excuse to justify my staring. I couldn't tear my eyes away from this beautiful, strong woman who made being a parent look easy and fun. "You're fine. Uh. I mean, I think your eyes are fine." *Smooth. Real smooth.*

She cleared her throat, and we both chuckled. "Ow," she grabbed her head. "It hurts to laugh."

I could understand that. "Are you dizzy? What about an ice pack?"

"I'm fine, really."

The paramedic that checked her out said she'd be fine, but I didn't like that her head hurt. "I think you're okay to lie down," I said. "I'll just hang on the couch. You won't even know I'm here."

"Like I could ignore you," she muttered, giving me a skeptical look and a once-over. My head almost touched the ceiling. I smiled easily, trying not to strut like a proud peacock back to the living area.

"Hey, that's the Pineapple fountain." A framed photo of Kami holding a baby Ryleigh in front of Charleston's iconic landmark sat beneath the lamp on the end table by the couch.

"Ryleigh's favorite swimming hole." She picked up the photo. "Gosh, I miss it there. I can't wait to go back."

"I hear ya. I don't know where my hockey career will take me, but I know I'll end up there when it's done. I can't imagine living out my life anywhere else." Home, for me, would always be by the sea. I loved the mountains, but I didn't want to live here forever.

"Same. I should have gone back after I got my bachelor's, but then Sutton got the transfer. We didn't think he would, so I wasn't prepared for it. I wish I'd listened to my gut. He wanted to get married so we could live on base together. When he got deployed, I was okay with it. I loved being alone. That should have been a sign. I had school and Brenna and my friends." Her confession held a regretful tone, almost resigned.

Did she feel guilty about not missing her husband? I wanted to know.

"You didn't miss him when he got deployed?"

She shook her head and sat on the couch. I lowered myself to sit next to her. "Not like the other wives. I genuinely like being alone, so it didn't seem odd, then. But looking back ... I didn't love him the way I should have. And he didn't love me that way, either. After we had Ryleigh, he, well, he—"

It was none of my business, but there was pain in her eyes, and I ached to soothe it. I wanted to know what she'd gone through and make sure it never happened again. "You don't have to tell me, but ... did he ... break his vows?" Her eyes met mine, and she didn't have to answer. "I'm so sorry."

"Not as sorry as I am. It was after Ryleigh was born, and I felt trapped. He promised it was a one-time thing, but it wasn't. Later I found out he'd had several affairs."

"That's horrible." I had no respect for cheaters.

"I always thought I was special. Worthy of selfless, unconditional love. I gave it, but I never received it. It was a hard lesson to learn. But I'm okay now. I've let go of impossible expectations, and if nobody comes around that loves the way I want to be loved, I'll stay single."

"You deserved to be loved, Kami. Cherished. He's a fool for letting you go." I wanted to take her in my arms and reassure her that she'd find the kind of love she wanted.

She shrugged and gave me a shy glance. It was adorable and tugged at my heartstrings the same way a sleeping Ryleigh did. "He wasn't the guy for me. That's all."

Her resilience and the ability to articulate that kind of wisdom seemed beyond her years. "Tell me about the guy for you." I swallowed, surprised at my forwardness. I'd try to lighten it up. "I've got a lot of great friends here. Maybe one of them is the guy for you."

Or maybe I was. Why not me? Though I felt the beginning of a spark between us, and I knew she felt it, too. But would she acknowledge it? And I was genuinely curious what she would say, and what she was looking for in a partner.

Slow down. Remember you swore off relationships. A broken heart stung, and I hadn't trusted myself to dive into the dating pool. After being used twice, I didn't want to put myself in the position of being made a fool of a third time. But Kami seemed different. She didn't take love lightly, and even with a cheating ex, she'd been faithful. There was no reason to think she'd burn me—except if she had a problem with distance. She'd mentioned going back to South Carolina, and unless I was sure it was absolutely going to work and we cared about each other equally, I wouldn't take a shot at getting burned again.

She laughed, a light tinkling sound I wasn't expecting. Staring at the picture still in her hands, she began to speak. "The guy for me would be my partner in every way. And I don't mean fifty-fifty. I mean one hundred percent combined, all the time. If I could only give twenty percent, he'd make up for it with eighty percent and vice versa. He'd be the very definition of kindness, never condescending, never patronizing or gaslighting. He wouldn't feel intimidated by my successes, and he'd support what I wanted to do and who I wanted to be. He'd... He'd ..." She paused and gave me a nervous smile. "Are you sure you want to hear all of this? Because I've got it all worked out in my head."

"I'm positive. Keep going." I didn't just want to hear this, I needed to know what she wanted in a partner. I needed to know if I was someone who could match her expectations.

"Okay, you asked for it." She took a deep breath and continued. "He'd make enough money or budget strategically so I could take time off to be with babies their first year. Or longer, if that's what the baby needed. I wouldn't have to work or worry who was going to watch my preschooler.

"He'd trust me, and I'd trust him. Completely. If he had to travel for work, I wouldn't have to worry that he'd be unfaithful, and he'd call me every day he was away, even if it was just to say I love you. He'd love Ryleigh like she was his own and spoil her rotten but also guide her firmly and help me instill a work ethic so she didn't grow up feeling entitled. He'd want to give her siblings."

"There's no doubt in my mind Ryleigh would be a doting big sister."

She looked up at me and smiled. "She would. The guy for me would be tall or wouldn't mind if I wore heels and made him look short. He'd never complain when I blasted or sang songs he didn't like, and *he'd* come to *me* to propose watching chick flicks and romantic comedies. He'd make the popcorn and cue up the movie." As she spoke, a blush rose from her neck to the apples of her cheeks. "And the guy for me would fight for love and our life together and never give up."

Long before she finished, I knew, without doubt, I wanted to be that guy.

"He's out there, Kami. Maybe hiding in plain sight."

She shook her head. "I don't even know if a guy like that exists. But I'd rather be alone than settle again."

"I'm with you on that." I didn't want to answer any questions, so I changed the subject. "Can I get you anything?"

"Nah. I'm going to go lie down now. I'm starting to feel sore all over."

"Okay. If you need anything—"

She patted my arm. "Thanks."

I settled back onto the couch and pulled out my phone to read. A little cuckoo clock near the kitchen chimed to mark the passing of time. Just after one o'clock, I began to nod off. Through the uncovered window behind Kami's bed, the falling white flakes glittered in the glow of an outside light.

Brenna hadn't texted me yet, so I sent her a message. *Everything okay at the restaurant?*

A few minutes later, her reply had me sitting up straight. *No. We lost power. I shooed all the customers out but I'm going to be a while.*

Are you by yourself?

Three bouncing dots appeared and then disappeared.

??? I texted back.

Brendan is here. He wouldn't leave.

Good man. Trotter had plenty of faults, but he'd seemed different lately, more serious and mature. Better on the ice, and off.

Yeah. Well. He seems handy, at least. We're going to get the generator from the old barn.

Okay. I can stay here till whenever.

Thanks.

Kami might not be happy when she woke up, but it was better for Brenna to be safe than try to brave the storm when I was already here. She had enough on her plate. And it made me feel better that she wasn't alone.

I put my phone on the coffee table and crossed the room to the front window. We were only expecting to get a few inches, but I'd been told by the locals that the bigger flakes were unpredictable. I peeked in on Ryleigh, who was sleeping soundly, and checked on Kami, who hadn't shifted since she'd lain down. Her even breathing was settling, and before I headed back to the couch, I checked to make sure the doors and windows were secured.

The small sofa wasn't made for six-foot-four humans to nap on, so I bent my knees over one end so I could at least lay my backside down. I stuffed a throw pillow under my head and found a fuzzy princess-themed blanket that was bunched up at the end of the couch to pull over my chest. I wasn't cold yet, but if the restaurant had lost power, Kami's house might, too. Eventually, I dozed off.

"Hey, that's my blankie! I need my blankie back!"

I blinked my eyes open to the blinding light of morning and a glaring Ryleigh. She stared me down like an inquisitor. "Ugh, sorry?" I tugged on the blanket and held it out as a peace offering.

Ryleigh sighed dramatically. "Why are you here, Mr. Tiggerman?"

"Um …" I looked over toward Kami's bed. She was still asleep in the same position. "Your mommy bumped her head really hard last night. She needs to rest. So I'm here to make sure you"—I booped her lightly on her nose with my finger—"are taken care of."

"Ohh." She looked toward her mom, then back at me. "Well, I can tell you how to do that."

"Do … what?"

"Take care of me." She booped me on the nose, and I grinned. "First, you make me breakfast. I like chocolate waffles with ketchup. Then we put on Thinter Bale movies.

Then, we play GAMES!" She giggled and jumped up and down, and I couldn't help laughing with her.

"Waffles with ketchup?" Had I heard her right?

"I don't like that sticky dippy sauce. Ketchup is waaaaaay better."

This kid sure was an original. "Okay, but you have to promise to be very quiet so your Mommy can rest, okay?"

"OKAY!" Her loud whisper was louder than her normal voice.

Ryleigh took my hand and pulled me into the kitchen, whisper-yelling all the way. A glance out the nearby window revealed the snow was still falling and we'd accrued over a foot of powder already.

I toasted her waffles, and she showed me where to find her special ketchup-dipping cup. I handed her the bottle, and she gleefully squirted the viscous red topping mostly into the tiny bowl.

The waffles popped up, and I put them on a plate.

"That's the wrong plate, Mr. Tiggerman."

"It is?"

She sighed dramatically and grabbed my hand, dragging me to a low cabinet next to the sink, where she flung open the door. Inside were stacks of fairy-themed cups, bowls, plates, placemats—you name it, it was in there.

I didn't want to pick the wrong plate twice. "Why don't you choose the one that's best for waffles?" I said.

She clapped and let go of me to retrieve a bright green plate with a bunch of fairies in the center. "This one!"

"Okay." I took it from her, transferred the waffles from the wrong plate, and popped two more into the toaster for me.

I picked up her ketchup and waffles and took it to the

table. She climbed up into a chair and fixed her brown eyes on me. "I can't eat these."

I blinked a few times. "Why not?"

"You didn't cut them."

"Ah. I can do that." I rummaged through a few drawers before I found a butter knife and returned to the table, where I proceeded to cut the waffle into square quarters.

"No!"

I jumped. Ryleigh's lower lip quivered. "That's *wrong*, Mr. Tiggerman."

Poor thing looked so serious. "Which way is right?"

"Pointy. So I can dip the corners of my ketchup."

"Hmmm." I scratched my chin. "How about I eat these, and I'll cut the next ones the right way, okay?"

"Okay. That will be good."

"My pleasure."

That made her giggle, and despite all the waffley hoops, I was really enjoying my time with her. After breakfast, I checked on Kami. Her breathing was low and even. This rest would do her good. Ryleigh and I played Candyland and watched movies for the next couple of hours. Kami slept through it all. Ryleigh and I checked on her a few more times. When the snow stopped around noon, I hunted around for a shovel and made her promise to stay on the couch until I came back in.

8

KAMI

*T*he front door clicked shut, and I slowly rolled my body over. Even the slightest movement sent daggers to my throbbing head. My neck was stiff, and I was certain I had a concussion.

I blinked wearily to pull the scene into focus. Ryleigh was on the couch, fully engrossed with her tablet. I'd heard Trask ask for the shovel, so I assumed he was outside.

That was nice of him.

My neighbors down the street usually sent their teenagers by to shovel, but by the time I'd been awake and conscious enough to read their texts, Ryleigh had told Trask about the shovel hanging from the hook on the front porch and he'd gone out.

I should probably let him know.

"Ry?" I hardly recognized my voice. Pressing my hands into the mattress, I attempted to raise my head.

Not gonna happen.

I sunk back into my pillow. "Ryleigh."

"Mommy! You're awake!" I closed my eyes and listened to

her run over to me and up the three steps to my bed. "Mr. Tiggerman is here!"

I winced. She was so loud. "I know, baby. Mommy's head hurts a lot. Can you whisper?"

"OKAY!" I winced again at the volume of her whisper. We'd have to work on that.

"Ryleigh, can you do something super-duper important for me?"

"YES!" It took all my effort not to cover my ears.

"Can you open the door to outside and tell Mr. Trask I would like to speak with him?"

"OKAY!"

I just about cried. *Deep breath, Kami.* I let my eyelids close again.

I pulled the pillow close to my ears and didn't ease up until I heard Trask's purposeful strides across the floor.

"Kami? How can I help?"

"Hey." I swallowed and opened my eyes. How different he was from Sutton. Not much in physical features; they were both well over six feet and muscular, with light hair and dark eyes. But that's where the similarities ended. Sutton relied on me to get things done and for emotional strength. Trask didn't need it. "The management company plows and shovels, but thank you. They should be along soon. You won't be stuck here all day. Promise."

"I don't mind."

I just about melted at his smooth response. I hadn't heard him speak with an accent until now, and it just hit me in all the feels.

"No need to cry, Kami." I didn't realize I was crying until his thumb brushed the corner of my eye. "How's your head?"

I couldn't form words but felt another tear leak out. Then another. And another.

He smiled but wasn't able to mask his concern. "That bad, huh? You want me to take you to get checked out?"

I squeezed my eyes shut. I didn't want to move to go anywhere. "Just … Can you grab me the bottle of ibuprofen?"

"Sure."

He brought me the bottle and a cup of water. "Thanks."

"You're welcome." Our gaze held. I couldn't look away. His concerned expression was the sweetest thing I'd seen in I couldn't remember how long.

"Um." Borderline awkward.

He shifted. "The boxes stacked in front of the TV labeled books—would you like me to unpack them for you? I can put together the bookcase, too."

I shook my head and grabbed it as the pain bounced like a pinball, hitting and lighting up every corner. "It's not attached."

At his blank expression, I explained further. "I'm waiting for Sutton—Ryleigh's dad—to come by and anchor the TV to the walls. The boxes are there so it doesn't fall on Ryleigh. He's also supposed to build and anchor the bookcase."

Trask broke our connection to look over at the mess of boxes by the TV. "If you have the stuff, I'm pretty handy."

I sighed. I had no energy to argue, and this was a nice favor. "Okay. But Ryleigh might want to help."

He grinned. "Great! I have just the job for her."

I smiled and relaxed into my bed. He seemed capable. And I needed rest.

It was nice to *rest*.

9

TRASK

Since hockey season started, I made it a habit to stop by Brewski's after practice. I went by every chance I could just to make sure Kami was all right. I was convinced she had a concussion, but she insisted that the rest she got the day after the accident was enough. By the night after the accident, she was functioning like nothing had happened. Her strength, willpower, and determination to get back out there were admirable.

We had Halloween off, so I stopped by Brewski's after lunch, when I knew she'd be working. I told her she had the heart of a hockey player.

"If that means I don't let a little injury keep me down, then thanks."

Kami's reaction to my compliment made me want to say everything that was on my mind, but I didn't want to overwhelm her. So I just winked instead.

"I'm going to engrave your name on that barstool," Kami joked as she handed me a menu.

I grinned and pointed to the wall, where the back panel of

a barstool hung with a fuzzy spiderweb stretched across it. "Like that one?"

"That's got Kingston's dad's name on it." She leaned forward. "Rumor has it that it broke when he jumped up on it the night Kingston was drafted."

I'd heard the story. My buddy—and former teammate —Kingston Brewer was Brenna's cousin and the nephew of the owners. It made sense his dad would have been here to watch the draft. I opened my mouth to comment but stopped when Kami's eyes slitted and her face tightened.

I turned to see what she was looking at. A man about my height stood by the hostess stand and frowned in our direction. I'd seen her ex here a few times before, each time dropping Ryleigh off when he was supposed to be watching her so Kami could work.

"Excuse me. I need to go find out why he's here. He wasn't supposed to pick her up from preschool this early."

Kami strode with purpose toward the entrance, and I slid off the stool to greet Ryleigh, who was headed in my direction bundled up in a big coat and carrying her Tinker Bell backpack.

"Mr. Tiggerman!" she wailed. It wasn't until I heard her voice that I realized she was upset.

"What is it?" I asked, crouching down to be eye level with her. "Are you okay?"

"No!" She gripped the straps of her backpack. "Daddy made me leave the Honnoh-ween party at school early!"

I glanced over to where Kami and Sutton were having a heated discussion. "I'm sorry about that. I'm sure he had a good reason."

"He said … he said … he forgoted. He has a meeting and he *forgotted* it. And we left before I got candy!"

Her little face wrinkled into a scrunch that I knew from experience with my niece preceded a full-on meltdown.

Maybe I could stop it.

I doubted that, but it was worth a shot.

I stretched out my hand and held her mittened fingers. "Do you like cherries?"

She sniffed and her lower lip shook, but she nodded.

"Okay. Let me have your backpack." I slid it off of her and set it on the floor. "I'm going to lift you up onto the stool, okay?"

She nodded and swiped at her eyes. I admired her effort to try to keep the tears in. "You can cry if you want to, Ryleigh," I said softly. "It's okay to be sad."

I lifted her into the seat of the stool I'd just vacated as she started to cry. Reaching over the counter, I took a napkin from the service side of the bar and used it to swipe a bunch of maraschino cherries, which I placed in front of her.

"All for you," I said, leaning on the bar next to her.

Her lips twitched and formed into a slow, unsteady smile. "Thank you."

"My pleasure," I drawled.

She giggled. "Grandpa Silly says that."

"Grandpa Silly?"

"My grandfather." Kami appeared on the other side of Ryleigh, visibly flustered. "He earned that nickname and wears it proudly."

"Sounds like my kind of guy," I said. I studied Kami's face. Her jaw muscles were twitching much the same as Ryleigh's had a few moments ago. "Are you okay?"

She shook her head and beckoned me behind the bar, speaking low so Ryleigh wouldn't overhear. "He was supposed to take her trick-or-treating! What am I going to tell her?"

Her stricken face knocked my heart straight into my gut. I dared to reach out and tip her chin up. Anguished watery eyes stared back at me, and I was even more determined to help her salvage Halloween for her little girl. "You tell her Mr. Tiggerman is going to take her."

Her lips parted in surprise, and her gaze darted to Ryleigh, who was staring at my phone like it was candy. I stretched to grab it and slid it into my pocket.

"You would do that for me?" Our eyes locked again, and I wondered if she felt the heat between us.

I would do so much more for her if she'd let me. Hopefully in time.

"Yeah. Ryleigh's a great kid. And we can tag along with Rurik and Craig's families. She knows their kids, right?"

"She does. Their daughters are in her class at school. Natasha and Ava are her besties." Her eyes twinkled as the plan formed. "And they'll all be here for Eat-Before-You-Treat." She nodded. "Okay. That's good. Very, very, good. Thank you, Trask." She launched herself at me, wrapping her arms around my waist and holding on tight.

I held her and closed my eyes. "It's my pleasure." My voice croaked.

A squeal from Ryleigh broke the tension. "Silly Tiggerman!"

Reluctantly, I left Kami behind the bar and went back to Ryleigh, bending down to chat with her. "How much did you overhear, Tinker Bell?"

"Everything!" She threw her arms around my neck and

kissed me smack on the nose, drooling a bit of sticky maraschino cherry juice. Kami hid a smile as she headed down the bar to greet new customers.

I laughed and settled her back on the stool. "Okay, then."

"What are you going to be tonight?" she asked.

"To be?" I wasn't following.

"*I'm* Thinter Bale. But *you*"—she pointed at my shirt—"are just a boy."

Ouch. I hoped her mother didn't share that opinion.

"So … you want me to dress up?" I glanced at the clock behind the bar. One o'clock. Plenty of time to pull my favorite costume out and get back here.

"It's a rule on Honnoh-ween," she said with a shrug.

And rules had to be kept.

10

KAMI

*B*y seven o'clock, Eat-Before-You-Treat had wrapped up, and my feet were killing me. Trask had left an hour earlier with the Antonovs and the Wards, after an impromptu photoshoot of the girls in front of the brewing equipment, which had been decorated for the event.

"Where's Ryleigh?" I jumped, my shoulders tightening at the familiar voice of Sutton Spencer. I froze, holding tightly to the soda glass and ice scoop. Anger boiled to the surface when I thought about how he'd let Ryleigh down, and I had to count to three before I turned around.

I felt Brenna behind me before she spoke. "She's trick-or-treating, Spencer. Where *else* did you think she'd be on Halloween night?"

"I'm supposed to take her. Why isn't she here?" he growled.

I glared at him. "Do I need to remind you how you unceremoniously and irresponsibly left her here this afternoon because *you* had better things to do?"

"I had a meeting!" he snapped. "I couldn't miss it. I told you I might make it back."

"Might is a far cry from *will*," I fired back. "What was more important than your daughter? You know how much she loves Halloween. How could you even think of ruining it for her?"

He ignored my question. "Who's she with?"

"My friends," I said through my clenched teeth.

He glared back at me. "Brenna is here. She going with Chelsea, then?"

I didn't answer.

"You're supposed to run any other babysitters by me before you let her go with anyone else."

"No, I don't." I seethed. "It's the other way around, since I have primary custody. Check your paperwork, Sutton. And next time, don't leave me in a pinch."

He squeezed his fists. "So who's she with?"

"Friends."

"Who?"

"What was so important?"

"Why don't you want to tell me?"

I stared him down, not willing to be the one to break this time.

"Hey, Kami, can Lauren and I get another round?" Jason sidled up next to Sutton and lifted his brows.

"Just a sec." I didn't break my gaze from Sutton.

"This guy giving you trouble?" Jason asked. *Bless him.*

"No more than usual," I said tightly.

Brenna smirked. "He was just leaving."

"Whatever." Sutton shrugged and backed away from the bar. "Not cool, Kamryn. I'll be checking that paperwork."

I let out a long breath, grateful he hadn't made a scene. The restaurant was busy, and I didn't want another public confrontation.

"Hey, you okay?" Jason asked. "That was your ex, right?"

"Yeah." My shoulders slumped as the tension eased out. "Sorry about that. I'll get your drinks right after I deliver these."

"Nah, we're good. Lauren's right at the snug window and sent me out here in case you needed help." He grinned. "But I see you and Brenna had it covered."

"It's like second nature to me." Brenna shrugged. "The first time I met him, he was visiting Kami at college, and he flipped out when he realized she and I had already had plans. We included him, of course, but he'd wanted to stay in all weekend with her, and made her feel guilty about it ruining his plans. I not so kindly reminded him that his last-minute dropping in ruined *our* plans."

"Maybe he missed you and wanted you all to himself?" Jason said to Kami before glancing toward the snug window and smiling at Lauren. She blew him a kiss.

"Don't go try making him sound all romantic," Brenna warned. "That guy only cares about himself. When I was helping her pack up to leave him, he freaked out because she wanted to take the microwave."

I winced. I was convinced it hadn't always been that way. It sure felt like it had, though. Sutton and I had started dating when I was a sophomore and he was a senior in high school. I still remembered our happier times. I hadn't wanted to get married so young, but after college—and his sixth year in the Air Force—it made sense. His transfer to Colorado Springs had been approved, and a marriage certificate was needed for us to live together in base housing.

He'd been gone a lot, and I'd been working on my master's degree. We'd wanted to wait until he had ten years in to have a baby, but Ryleigh had surprised us, in every good way. It had been hard when he was deployed, but I'd made it work. The base had day care, so I'd leave her there while I went to class. I didn't have much time to make friends, but Brenna was local and she was enough. Sometimes I felt like Ryleigh and I were burdens, like the night I slid off the road, but Brenna reminded me I'd do the same if our situations were reversed.

A little after nine, I was cashing out at the register near the hostess stand when Trask and Ryleigh returned. He was dressed as a pirate, sans hat, with a heavy colonial-style burgundy coat and ruffled shirt peeking out under his neck. He held Ryleigh in his arms, and she wiggled to be put down when she saw me.

"Mommy! Look!" In her hands, she clutched her candy bag. "It got filled three times! Mr. Tiggerman said I got the mostest Honnoh-ween candy he's ever saw!"

I put down my receipts and scooped her up into my arms. She was so fidgety I wondered how much of that candy she'd already consumed. "Wow! That's amazing! Did you thank him for taking you?"

She placed her mittened hands on my cheeks and rolled her eyes. I quirked a brow. That was new.

"Of course, Mommy! I said thank you every time he said trick-or-treat to the scary people and every time he called me pretty."

I snorted and snuck a peek at Trask. His sheepish grin did funny things to my insides.

He shook his head. "You wouldn't believe how many people wear scary costumes to give out candy. Poor kids were terrified."

"Thank you again for taking her. You saved Halloween." Ryleigh yawned, and I hugged her closer. "Let Mommy go get her things and then I'll take you home, okay?"

"Okay." She twisted and reached for Trask. He caught her, and she rested her head on his shoulder. My heart melted when her thumb found its way into her mouth, a sign of contentment and trust. "Mistah Tiggahrshman?" she asked, her thumb still in her mouth.

"Yeah, Tinker Bell?" he whispered.

Be. Still. My. Heart.

"Can you read me a goodnight story?"

I sucked in a breath. Trask looked at me, and I nodded.

Whoa.

Just whoa. I mentally ticked off all the ways he'd already impressed me today. And now Ryleigh was requesting a bedtime story ... that was huge. Trask seemed too good to be true, albeit genuine.

"I need to, um—" I looked around, as if I could find words when my pulse was racing a mile a minute as this huge, wonderful, handsome guy cradled my now-sleeping baby to his chest.

"Go ahead and get your stuff, Kami. I've still got your keys. I'll get her into her car seat and then I can follow you home."

I nodded and raced to the break room, past Brenna's quizzical look, and was out the side door and back at my car before a rational thought—like not wanting a relationship with this man—could take hold in my brain.

As I turned the corner onto our street, my stomach sank at the familiar car parked in front of the house. I glanced in the rearview mirror. Ryleigh was asleep, and Trask was still behind me.

This wasn't good.

I pulled into the driveway and jumped out, leaving the car running and lifting a silent prayer that Ryleigh wouldn't wake up to see her parents fighting again. Trask pulled in behind me as Sutton got out of his car.

The next few minutes passed in a blur. Trask hopped out of his truck and was by my side before Sutton could reach me. When he did, he glared at Trask before launching into his usual abusive rhetoric.

This time, though, he went too far.

"So you and this jock, huh?" He jerked his thumb and turned to face Trask. "You trying to steal my family?"

"Steal your—what the heck, Sutton!" I shook with anger. "First, he's a friend. Second, you're the one who broke up this family. Carlotta's what? Your fourth girlfriend? Third, he's here to read Ryleigh a bedtime story." Saying that out loud, I realized how lame it sounded. "Fourth … fourth …" I stuttered, unsure of what to say next.

He didn't deserve an explanation, especially after cheating on me. Now, because I had a *friend*, he was concerned about his family?

"Fourth"—Trask glanced at me before continuing—"it's none of your damn business what I'm doing here."

Sutton stepped closer to Trask and held his head up so that they were eye to eye. I glanced at the car window. Ryleigh was still sleeping, thank goodness.

"Everything she does with my kid is my damn business." Sutton's clenched fists indicated this was going to escalate quickly if I didn't intervene.

"Sutton, you need to go. Now," I said.

"You don't tell me what to do." He spoke to me but didn't divert his attention from Trask. They'd be an even match if they started fighting. I didn't want to see that.

"Sutton," I said again, this time gently. "Please stop. You'll scare Ryleigh. I know you don't want her to be afraid of you."

He took a step back, and I saw clarity in his eyes. "Fine. We'll talk about this another time." He turned back to Trask. "Watch yourself."

Trask pressed his lips together but didn't respond. We watched Sutton return to his car and drive away. I stood, frozen and shaking, not from the cold, while Trask turned off the car, retrieved Ryleigh from it, and carried her to the front door.

The picture of him in a long eighteenth-century coat standing on my stoop, weighed down by my sleeping daughter, her Halloween bags on one shoulder and my tote bag on the other, would be forever burned into my brain as one of the most endearing images I'd ever seen.

11

TRASK

"Your guests are here," Brendan announced as we waited for our cue to skate out for our next home game. "Do you think if I gave Brenna a jersey she'd wear it?"

"Never know till you ask," I replied. I pushed past him and peeked out of the tunnel. I'd gotten Kami, Ryleigh, and Brenna tickets at the glass. I wanted to be able to skate by and high-five Ryleigh if I scored.

There they were, wearing jerseys with my number on them. I felt a weird sensation bubble up inside me and swallowed it down. I hadn't been this nervous to play in a game since my first time on ice with the Voltage.

This was no time for jitters.

It had been a week since Halloween. That night, I'd stayed at Kami's just long enough to read to Ryleigh. I picked up on the signs that she needed some time to be alone, and I didn't want to overstay my welcome. I didn't understand Kami's relationship with Sutton. Sometimes it seemed amicable, other times explosive. I was glad they split up. She was way too good for him.

And as caveman-ish as it might sound, I wanted to protect them from Sutton's nonsense.

I'd only stopped by Brewski's once this week and on impulse invited her and Ryleigh to the game. I didn't want her to think that her ex had spooked me, but the truth was, the confrontation on Halloween had made me uncomfortable and I wondered if I should back off a little. Deep down, I felt an overwhelming need to protect Kami and Ryleigh, but I didn't know the ins and outs of their relationship with Sutton. And the last thing I wanted was to make more problems for Kami.

"Please get on your feet for your Voltage starting lineup!"

The announcer's voice took me out of my thoughts. *Here we go.* Taking a deep breath, I followed the offensive line out of the tunnel and onto the ice. I pushed off my left skate and sailed out to greet the six-thousand-plus fans in attendance at tonight's game. I had a good feeling about this one. The Utah Arches had had more lineup changes than us during the off-season, and we were favored to win—if we could get it together.

"At right wing, number fifty-six, Rurik Antonov! Center-man, number twenty-five, Maddox Knott! At left wing, number thirty-seven, Andrej Lindt. At your home blue line, number eleven, Trask Emerson, and number ninety-eight, Brendan Trotter. And in goal, the captain of your Palmer City Voltage, number eighty-eight, Jaaaaaaaaaason Dexter!"

Maddox won the face-off, and Andrej took possession of the puck, weaving through the opposing players and over their blue line. Coming up against a defenseman, he spun around and passed the puck to Rurik, who was open on the left side of the net. Two Utah players headed straight for him, and I skated toward him for backup.

The four of us battled for control of the puck against the wall, and I got an elbow to my rib. As I caught my breath, the whistle blew. We broke apart and moved into position for a face-off. Rurik nodded to me, then set for the drop.

I was ready. We needed the win to tie for first in the points standings, and I was determined to play my best tonight. Rury won control and sent the puck straight to my waiting stick. I skated hard for the net and saw my opening. I slid into position for a wrist shot and hit the puck, sending it sailing towards the net. The goalie caught it in his glove, and I shook my head as I skated back to our bench.

"Good try, Mr. Tiggerman!"

I looked up to see Ryleigh in her mother's arms, clapping for me. The gesture and encouragement hit me straight in my heart. I grinned and winked at her as I lifted my stick in a wave. I slid through the gate and dropped to the bench next to Brendan.

He lifted his glove for a fist bump. "Nice shot. You'll get it next time. Their goalie isn't at his best today. He's playing hard out of the gate, overcompensating, probably because he's hungover. He'll tire out."

"Oh yeah?" I squinted to look at the Utah goalie. "How do you figure? He looks to be in top form to me."

Brendan shook his head. "We played together in Juniors. He's starting out hard. Guaranteed he'll lose steam towards the end of the second period. He's new to this team, so they may not realize his tells yet. If they don't pull the backup in after the second intermission, we can get a good rally going and they won't even know what hit them."

True to Brendan's prediction, the goalie played hard but tired out, and by the third period, the Arches were up 2-0.

"Line change!" Coach barked. "Emerson, Trotter, do not let another shot near Dexter! Antonov, Lindt, Knott—we need shots on goal. Do your job!"

We climbed over the wall and joined the starting offensive line. Rurik got possession of the puck, and Brendan and I followed him over the red line. Rurik passed it to Maddox, who took a shot. The goalie cleared it, but I could tell he was moving more slowly around the crease.

Andrej stole the puck from their winger and whipped it over to me. I saw an opening and took my shot. It slid past the goalie's skate and into the net. I raised my stick in celebration as the lamp lit up, registering the goal.

Brendan appeared next to me and we jumped at each other for a celebratory chest bump. The crowd cheered as my teammates skated over and patted me on the back. I broke away to skate by Kami and Ryleigh. I owed her a high five.

I placed my glove on the glass, and Kami held her up. Ryleigh hit the glass and giggled. "Do it again, Mr. Tiggerman!" I winked at her, and she blew kisses at me as I skated away.

They were still watching me as I slid back onto the bench. Unlike my last two girlfriends, who'd hardly paid attention to the game, Kami was into it. Every time I looked their way, her eyes were either on me or the puck.

The way that made me feel … I didn't have words to describe it.

I scored again and repeated the new ritual. High five, wink, air kisses.

Scoring wasn't the best feeling ever. Having people you wanted to share it with was.

KAMI

"*I*'m sorry, Mama. I just can't manage it." I huddled in the corner of the bar with Brenna's phone to my ear.

It was the Saturday night before Thanksgiving. My mother had reached out to Brenna because I hadn't returned her calls for days. I'd been avoiding this inevitable conversation, regretting to have to tell her that Ryleigh and I wouldn't be home for Christmas this year, nor would she be home with her dad as planned for Thanksgiving.

Sutton was supposed to have her for Thanksgiving, and he called yesterday to ask if I could take her since he'd been invited to a "thing" with a group of co-workers and no one else had kids. I'd had plans to spend the long weekend checking soil samples and reading journal articles for data comparison. I'd found something that didn't make sense in the data, and I needed to revisit my sites in the mountains to collect more soil samples before I could finish this part of my dissertation.

Luckily, Brenna had the Saturday off and said she could

stay with Ryleigh overnight. She'd wanted me to tell Sutton he didn't get to choose when to be a father and when not to be, but truthfully, I wanted Ryleigh with me. I had to work Thanksgiving and would check my soil samples on Saturday, and with Brenna's help, both were doable. Sutton had been acting stranger and stranger, and the thought of him taking Ryleigh for a long weekend concerned me in a way I couldn't explain.

"But honey, we want to see you and support you. You know we can't leave to come see you, or we'd be there in a heartbeat."

I felt bad. I really did. But even with the excessive tips from Trask and his friends and low living costs, I wasn't able to afford the trip. The alternator had eaten up the flight money, but it wasn't just the cost of airfare I had to worry about. My family would want me to stay until the new year, and I'd miss a week or more of work, which was the deciding factor.

My parents were in no position to help me. My family ran an apiary outside Charleston, selling queen bees and packages of bees. They supplemented their income growing and selling honey and exotic greenery from their small nursery at local farmers markets and plant sales. Missing a weekend, especially a holiday weekend, would be just as bad for them as it would be for me if I couldn't work.

I couldn't wait until I had a salaried job.

"I know, Mama." I sighed. "How are Mimi and Pop Pop? And Grandpa Silly?"

She chuckled. "I can never hear that nickname enough. I've been telling my daddy all my life how silly he is and it just tickles me that his great-granddaughter was the one to dub that nickname!"

I giggled. "Yeah, I can't ever call him Grandpa Wally anymore."

"Oh no. Never." I missed my mother's musical laugh. I'd lived in Colorado for nine years, but my home and heart would always be in South Carolina. I couldn't wait to go home with my PhD and live out the rest of my life there.

Notes of deep male voices caught my ear, and I turned toward the entrance. A slew of Voltage players filed in, fresh off another home game win in a row. As they headed for the function room, one broke off from the group, and my cheeks reddened as the familiar, tall, handsome defenseman headed straight toward me.

"Mama, I really gotta go. The players just came in ..." I trailed off as Trask dropped into the seat at my end of the bar, his damp hair falling across his forehead as he removed his hat.

"Okay, honey. But you'll let me know if your plans change?" The wistful tinge in her voice hurt my heart.

"I will. But I just can't make the numbers work this year. I still have fees—" I caught Trask's eye and lowered my voice. "I really wish I could come home for Christmas, too. I need you to understand how sorry I am."

"I do, baby. I do." She blew out a breath. "Okay, well, we'll send gifts and video chat, and I'll be counting the days until your graduation ceremony. Your daddy and I will be there. Come hell or high water."

"Okay. I love you. Tell Daddy I love him, too. We'll video-call you on Thanksgiving, okay?"

"Okay, baby girl. I love you, too."

I ended the call and stared at the phone. I jumped when Trask cleared his throat.

"Sorry," I apologized, sliding Brenna's phone into my apron pocket. "Congrats on your win tonight."

"Thanks. It was a good one. Wish you had been there."

Our eyes locked, and my cheeks were now burning. It was obvious from the adoring way he looked at me how sweet he was on me. Trask was a ray of sunshine in my stormy life, and that look always brightened me up. I couldn't remember the last time Sutton looked at me like that. Come to think of it, I wasn't sure he'd ever looked at me like that.

I liked him, too, more and more every time I saw him. He was turning into a really great friend. I couldn't think about wanting more, though. I was so close to being done in Colorado. A relationship between us could never work.

But ... No. I didn't think I was ready for another relationship. But I liked Trask, and Ryleigh liked him, too. I was enjoying getting to know him. If something was in the cards for us, it would come together on its own and present a clear sign.

He cleared his throat, and I realized I hadn't responded. "I'd definitely like to take Ryleigh to another game sometime." That was lame. True, but lame.

"Just let me know when. I'll text you the schedule."

"Okay." I gestured to the bar behind me. "What can I get you?"

"Um ... I couldn't help overhearing that last part ... about you not going home for Christmas?"

My eyes snapped to his. They shone with sincerity, and there was no reason to not talk to him about this. I nodded.

"Well ..." He rubbed the back of his neck.

Was he nervous? I leaned in, and my heart thudded against the bar in anticipation of what he was going to say.

"Well?" I prompted.

He suddenly grinned. "My sister is getting married on December twenty-third. Would you and Ryleigh like to be my dates? I'll cover your flights. It's at this bee farm right outside Charleston."

I gasped. *No freaking way.*

"Ellis's Bee Farm?" I squeaked. It couldn't be.

But it could.

OhmyGod.

"Yeah. You know it?"

I chuckled, and then the chuckle turned into a laugh, and then the tears came. I barely noticed Brenna return to the bar. I gave her back her phone and swiped at my eyes. I probably looked a mess, but I really didn't care.

Talk about a clear sign. Yeesh.

Poor Trask. His confused expression was priceless. And adorable.

"What did you say to her?" Brenna asked.

He shrugged. "Just that my sister was getting married at a bee farm."

Her eyes widened, and she looked at me. *"Ellis's* Bee Farm? In Summerville?"

"Yeah. You know it, too?"

"Of course I do." Brenna looked at me. "You didn't tell him?"

I wiped my eyes. I had to get myself together. With the cost of flights at the holidays plus missed time off work, I hadn't even considered making a trip this year. But if he covered the flights, it was doable. *What a gift.* I forced a smile.

"Haven't had the chance. I'm sorry I reacted like this, Trask. Oh, wow. Yes, Ryleigh and I would love to be your dates to your sister's wedding." I couldn't wait to call my mother later and let her know we were back on for a family Christmas.

"Even if it's at a bee farm? I know it sounds unusual, but she says the bees are separate from where the guests are allowed, and it's the prettiest venue around."

"Oh, it definitely is," Brenna said. "Kami's family owns it. Her maiden name is Ellis."

"No freaking way!" Trask's grin was so big, I just wanted to hug him. "I think I would have reacted the same way. That's so cool."

"It is. My sisters have done a great job of sprucing up the old barn and surrounding area over the last couple years. It's gorgeous." It really was. If I ever got married again ... *stop that thought dead in its tracks, Kamryn.*

Brenna leaned on the bar. "So gorgeous, after I saw it, I decided to do something similar with our old barn. If I can get it cleared soon and find a reliable contractor, I'm hoping to be doing weddings out back by the end of next summer."

"That's great, Brenna." Trask nodded toward the function room and grinned. "Trotter mentioned helping you clean it out."

"Yeah, yeah. Speaking of." She turned back to me. "I need to get those days figured out. Thanksgiving, you're working, and I'm dining with Ryleigh. Friday, you're off and I'm working. Saturday, I've got Ryleigh while you head out to collect your soil samples, and I'll stay over since you'll be back super late. Is it okay if I take her to the barn? The team is off that day, and Brendan said he can round up a few guys to help get the big items out."

"Yeah, that's fine. I really appreciate you taking her, Brenna."

"I've told you so many times—I love that kid." She pulled me into a side hug. "I'm happy to help."

"I know," I whispered. "You're the best." I turned back to Trask as she scooted off. "So what can I get you?"

"Just water. Where's Ryleigh tonight?"

"She's with her dad this weekend." I picked up a glass, scooped ice, and grabbed the hose to fill it up. When I handed it to him, our eyes met, and I quickly let go.

"That's cool. What do you have planned for tomorrow?"

Was that a leading question? I wished I had nothing planned so I could find out. "Reading. I noticed a discrepancy in my research, and I need to nail it down before I head into the mountains next Saturday to recollect some samples at my sites. I need to verify some data."

He nodded and leaned back in his seat. "That's cool. So are you a geologist, then? What do you want to do when you get your PhD?"

"Earth science. Soil and the effects of weather on structure and formation, specifically, and in turn how that affects plant growth. I've always been fascinated with all the different soil groups and map units in the Lowcountry. The mountain soils are so different from the marshy and clay types in the South. Choosing to get my degree here widens my scope of knowledge. But eventually, I'd really like to teach college students back home."

"I hear ya. There's no place like the Lowcountry." His expression turned serious, and suddenly I felt like we were the only people in the restaurant.

"No." My breath hitched as a warm tingle made its way up my arms to my shoulders. "No, there isn't."

"Nothing like it," he said softly.

I shivered as our gazes held. "I should, um, check in on the function room." Servers had brought out the catering that had been called in ahead of time, but it was my room to oversee and work. I'd only meant to step out of the room for a minute to take my mother's call.

He raised his glass of water and slid from the stool. "I'll see you in there."

"See you in there," I whispered.

Lordy. It was getting harder and harder to pretend I just wanted to be friends with him.

13

TRASK

"*M*r. Tiggerman!"

I'd barely stepped into Brewski's on Thanksgiving when I heard Ryleigh calling for me. I traced her voice to a table on the wall that bordered the function room. She stood up on her seat and was quickly steadied by Brenna.

Behind me, Jason snorted. We'd driven over together since Lauren was coming with her brother, who was the Voltage's equipment manager.

"Shut it," I warned him as we checked in at the host stand.

"I think the little lady has a crush on you," he replied.

I ignored him as the hostess led us to a table opposite the long table occupied by Brenna's family and Ryleigh. I swept the room looking for Kami but didn't see her.

"Hey, guys." Brenna waved. "Come meet my cousin Liam!"

"Hey." I left Jason at our table and greeted the Brewer family. I offered my hand and introduced myself just as Ryleigh launched herself over Brenna and into the man's lap to try to get to me.

"Sorry, Mr. Liam!" Ryleigh reached up for me, and I hoisted her into my arms. "Auntie Brenna, can I pleeeeeeeeease sit with Mr. Tiggerman? Or Natasha?"

I glanced back at Jason. Lauren had just arrived with her brother and his family. Behind them, Rurik and his family were settling in at a nearby table.

"Please?" The little girl blinked with an expression that could teach puppy dogs a thing or two. "There are no fun people at my table!"

We laughed. "Is that so?" I asked.

"Yes! They keep talking about Auntie Brenna's barn. SO boring!"

"Sorry, kid." Liam shrugged. "I'm only in town for the weekend," he explained to me. "We need to get it cleared so I can evaluate the structure and draw up plans for the reno."

"Liam's an architect," Brenna explained.

"So Saturday's the day then? I haven't heard from Trotter." I glanced around. "Is he coming today, or did he fly back to Minnesota for Thanksgiving?" That would be a heck of a travel schedule. We played yesterday and had an afternoon game tomorrow.

"He's coming later. I haven't asked him yet." Her cheeks reddened. Maybe Trotter wasn't as much of a pest as I thought.

"Trask!" My head snapped to Ryleigh, who'd never called me by just my first name before. She grabbed my cheeks and pulled my face so that it was almost touching hers. "Pleeeease can I sit with you?"

A titter of laughter and I felt my own face reddening. "Tell you what. Let's go ask Natasha's mommy and daddy if you can sit with them, okay?"

She sighed dramatically. "Okay."

A few minutes later, we'd pulled our tables together at Rurik's suggestion to create one larger party. Craig and Svetlana Ward and their daughter joined us. Ava was also in Ryleigh's class, and the three little girls were soon chattering away.

I craned my neck and finally spotted Kami on the other side of the restaurant. I couldn't remember the last time I'd been here that she wasn't our server. I caught her eye a few times during the meal and warmed every time her shy smile returned mine.

Finally, during dessert, she stopped by our table. "How's my girl doing?" she asked Ryleigh but looked in my direction.

"I'm mad," Ryleigh said matter-of-factly. "So mad."

"You are?" Kami glanced at me, confused. I shrugged. I'd been deep in conversation with Lauren's brother and hadn't been paying attention to the girls' chatter.

"Yes!" Ryleigh's lower lip trembled. "I have to go to the dirty old barn Saturday so I can't see Santa!"

"Santa?" Kami knitted her brows.

"The Santa Express!" Dmitri, Natasha's five-year-old brother, looked up from his tablet and bounced in his seat. "We wear our pajamas and go on the train, and we drink hot chocolate and the train brings us to Santa's workshop!"

"It's so fun," Natasha said. "And Ava and her mommy and daddy are coming, too."

Kami closed her eyes, but I saw the pain in them before they closed. I knew she couldn't miss her research day. I hated that she was a single mom and had to constantly make choices between Ryleigh and work.

"What if I took her?" I blurted before I could think. All the heads at the table turned to look at me, including Kami's. She looked surprised.

Crap. I should not have said that in front of Ryleigh. If Kami said no, she'd look like the bad guy.

Ryleigh squealed. "Pretty please, Mommy? I'll be the goodest girl *ever!*"

Kami looked back and forth between me and Ryleigh. "Um ..."

"We'll keep an eye on them." Kira winked at me, her accent thick to my overworked ears. "No trouble. Ryleigh *is* good girl. Just pack a bag, dress her in jammies, and we will all watch her and make sure she has fantastic time. Yes?"

Ryleigh stood on her chair and wrapped her arms around her mother's waist. "Pleeeeeeesh?" she muffled, rubbing her face into Kami's shirt.

"You're sure you don't mind?" Kami asked me. "What about helping Brenna at the barn?"

"I'd love to," I said. And I meant it. This little girl had taken up as much space in my heart as her mother had. "I can help another time if Trotter can't find enough hands."

"Okay, then. I'll talk to Auntie Brenna, Ryleigh."

"Yay!" Ryleigh squeezed her mom harder, and Kami kissed the top of her head. A tear leaked out of the corner of her eye, and it hit me right in the gut. Was she sad she couldn't come? Or about something else?

I wouldn't ask. I would make sure Ryleigh had the best damn time possible on the Santa Express.

But right now, I had an important stop to make.

I said my goodbyes, promised Ryleigh I'd see her soon, and headed out to my truck. On the front seat, I adjusted the large bag from Sunflower Bakery to make sure it didn't slide while I drove. I fussed with the pink bow that tied the handles together. Doing so reminded me I hadn't called my parents yet today.

As my truck warmed up, I dialed my mother's number. She picked up on the first ring. "Hey, Mama. Happy Thanksgiving."

"Hey, baby. I miss you."

"I miss you, too. How are you feeling?"

"Better now that you called. You know it's a day-to-day thing."

"Yeah." And I felt guilty on the days I didn't call. I was always afraid of how she might sound, and that messed with my mind on game days. How could I play hockey when I knew my mother was suffering? So most days, I texted her.

"Did you go by the house yet?" she asked. The house was an old mauve-colored Victorian on the edge of Palmer City, just a short walk from the cancer treatment center. A foundation funded the room and board of patients who were too far from home to drive in regularly or had no support system. Our family had often visited the one near us, and I'd picked up the tradition when I moved to Palmer City.

"I'm on my way there now."

"Those are some lucky ladies, Trask. I'm so proud of you for the time you spend there and for your gifts to them. I know you'd do the same if you were here."

"I would."

We chatted a little bit longer, and then I pulled out of the lot. Carnation House was about a half hour's drive away in Colorado Springs. I pulled into the circular driveway and parked in front of the entrance. I didn't plan to stay today, and

I knew if I parked there, Joy, the owner, would hustle me out for blocking the driveway.

I rang the bell, and seconds later, Joy flung open the door and flashed me a wide grin. "Trask Emerson, aren't you looking fine today!" She stared up at me through black-rimmed glasses as I returned the grin. At least eighty, round, and barely five feet tall, she was a ray of sunshine on this cold winter day in her flowery print dress.

"As are you, Ms. Joy. Fine as a sunny summer day. You're wearing a dress."

She waved her hand. "No need for concern. You know I get dressed up three times a year. Thanksgiving, Christmas, and Easter. We've had this conversation before."

"We have. But I had to tell you anyway."

"You flatter me. But I like it." She shot me a pointed look. "You gonna come in?"

"Not today. But I brought dessert."

She leaned to the side to look past me. "What'd I tell you about blocking the driveway?"

I shrugged and winked. "I was hoping you'd forgive me when you opened the bag."

"Oh, really? Awful bold of you to presume." She raised her eyebrows in challenge.

"So it was wrong of me to ask the bakery to include a separate dozen red velvet petit fours?" I frowned. "I guess I'll have to eat them myself."

"You will do no such thing, and you know it. Hand them over." She stuck out her hand for the bag, and I gave it to her. She peeked inside. "There are three boxes of the red velvet petit fours."

"Must have been an ordering mistake." I shrugged.

"That's too much, Trask."

"For what you do for these women? It's not even close to being enough. And I know their families would agree with me if they could be here. It's Thanksgiving. And we're all grateful to you."

She set the bag down and wrapped her arms around my waist. "You're a gift, Trask Emerson. Thank you."

14

KAMI

"We'll be fine! Go!" Brenna waved her hand at me as I paused in the doorway for what felt like the tenth time. My heart knew her words were true, but my mind wrestled with the sheer amount of trust I was putting into Trask. What if something happened to Ryleigh and I wasn't there?

"But—" I glanced at my daughter, snuggled up on the sofa in her Tinker Bell nightgown and pink Santa hat with a plastic sparkly tiara hot-glued to the front above the white furry cuff. In her arms, she clutched a plush Belle doll dressed in her Christmas gown. Unable to find such a thing last Christmas, I called my sister Khloe and asked her to custom-make the burgundy and gold outfit for a stuffed version I'd found of Ryleigh's favorite princess.

I should be taking her to this, or at least her father should. I felt like the worst slacker parent. It was already noon, and if I didn't leave soon, I'd make Brenna late for the meeting with her cousin Liam.

"But nothing. Get out of your head." Brenna's expression

softened. "I know you want to go, but eyes on the prize, okay? You've got to finish your research. After this weekend, you may not get the chance until the ground thaws in a few months."

"You're right," I conceded, hanging my head. The tools I had access to for sampling wouldn't do well on frozen ground. It was now or never. I sighed. "You're sure you've got this? And you'll be available if anything happens?"

"You *know* I will, Kam." She smiled. "Let's go over this one more time. You're taking my car." She handed me her keys. "I'm meeting Liam, Brendan, and whatever friends he has at the barn with Ryleigh at twelve thirty. Trask will pick her up there at one o'clock for the Santa train ride and leave me his truck. I'll buckle Ryleigh into her car seat, and he'll take your car to the train station. Boarding is at two o'clock. They'll return to the station by seven, he'll drop Ryleigh and your car off here afterward, and she and I will snuggle in for the night until you get back. Did I miss anything?"

"No." I adjusted my backpack on my shoulder. It was heavy and awkward with all the gear I'd need to collect soil samples at my sites. Many of the tools didn't exactly fit and stuck out of the top of my pack. I would have preferred to go earlier in the morning, but Brenna had gotten called in to help with the breakfast rush at Brewski's. I'd assured her I'd still have plenty of time before sunset to do most of what I needed to do, and as a precaution I'd save my easiest-to-access site for last. She already helped me so much I didn't mind working around her schedule.

"Then I'll see you tonight, Kami. *Don't worry.*" She gently pushed me out the door.

I nodded. "Okay. See you tonight."

The drive out to the sites was pleasant. It was a mild late November day, by Colorado standards. Back home, if it got this cold, we'd be huddled up indoors by a fire and layered up in our warmest clothes.

I was still layered up, but I liked the brisk mountain air. It was rejuvenating, clear, and fresh, a direct contrast to the heavy, muggy, humid warmth of the Lowcountry in South Carolina.

I was appreciative of the little "heat wave" we'd had this week. It had melted the snow enough so as to keep my sites accessible, and at the same time, it offered an added bonus to my research on how weathering affected the soil.

As I trudged up the path to my first site, I tried to clear my head and focus on my work. When I reached the glen where I'd first decided to focus my dissertation on weathering patterns on soil structure and texture, I stood for a moment to take in the surroundings and fight back memories of happier, easier times.

Sutton and I had found this spot on one of our first hikes when we'd moved here. All it needed was a Tudoresque cottage to make it a storybook setting. It even had a quaint bubbling brook. In the summertime, it was lush with vegetation: pines, birch, and wildflowers rich in color and variety. Now, the birch and other deciduous trees had shed their leaves. The grass had lost its green hue, and the water in the brook reflected a gray sky, unlike the vibrant blue of a clear summer day.

But had they been happier and easier? Or did I just tell myself that because that's what I wanted to think?

Sutton had been gone a lot, first on deployments and then classified "projects," which I suspected weren't work-related, but I couldn't prove it. We'd done okay financially, and I'd been able to stay at home with Ryleigh while I took classes. I was able to drop her off and pick her up from the day care on base myself and hadn't had to rely on Brenna or friends for anything.

Sutton wasn't a social guy, not like Trask, who had a big team of friends he spent time with on and off the ice. I was sure Sutton was close to men in his unit, but he never talked about them, and we never had people over. I hadn't made any extra effort to connect with other wives and mothers on base, except for an occasional kid's birthday party if Ryleigh was invited.

Life was changing fast, maybe faster than what I was ready for.

I set my backpack down and opened it to retrieve my shallow auger, a Ziploc bag, and a trowel. About six feet from the water, I located the original site I'd previously sampled. I cleared the loose vegetation and pushed the auger into the ground. It wasn't easy, since the recent snowfall had hardened the ground, but at least it wasn't frozen. It took even more muscle to pull the auger out, but I managed. With the bag in one hand, I knocked the soil out of the auger. Squeezing the bag between my fingers, I mixed the soil before setting it aside.

I had my hand lens with me but decided to wait until I got back home to analyze the sample. I'd borrowed a 10x microscope from the lab and planned to spend most of my day off Monday double-checking particle size and crystalline structure. Today, I just needed to get the soil.

I labeled the bag with a permanent marker and continued up the trail, wishing I was with my girl on the Santa Express. I told myself for the millionth time there would be plenty more opportunities once I had my doctorate and my financial concerns were a thing of the past.

I knew when I moved us out of base housing that it would strain our finances. I'd been okay for a while getting by on my savings, but when they ran low, I panicked. Brenna offered me a job, but that meant I needed regular day care. The base day care was too far for Brenna to help out, so on her suggestion, I enrolled Ryleigh in the Plex's pre-kindergarten program for three-year-olds. Then Ryleigh met the Kriz twins and got hooked on cheer after a free class.

Now that hockey season had started up, I was making enough money at Brewski's when I worked home game nights and team events. There was always a big crowd when the team played in town, and the fans were big drinkers and big tippers. It helped that Brenna's brother Keegan was working on expanding the brewery part of the business and gave free samples every few weeks when he had a new flavor to test out.

I finished up at the first site and packed my gear up. I'd estimated about eight hours and was right on schedule. If I kept this pace, I'd be home around her bedtime, and maybe Trask would still be there.

15

TRASK

"*R*yleigh? You okay in there?" I stood outside the bathroom as the Santa Express chugged back toward Palmer City. It'd been about five minutes, and I was beginning to get a bad feeling.

"I'm okay!"

A few more minutes passed, and I knocked again. "Do you need help?"

"No! Um, yes! But—no! I need Mommy's bag!"

Kami's bag was about ten rows away. I sprinted for it and was back in record speed, despite the confused looks from my friends and other passengers.

"I have it. Can you open the door?"

The doorknob turned, and Ryleigh poked her head out, revealing just enough of herself to not reveal too much. The unmistakable aroma of number two wafted out. I looked past her into the tiny compartment.

Ryleigh stuck her hand out for the bag.

"Hold on a sec, sweetie." I crouched down so I was eye level with her. "Do you need help?"

"Um." She turned to look behind her, then hung her head. "My bum is super poopy. Mommy or Auntie Brenna or Daddy or my teacher always makes it clean."

Good lord. "It's okay, Ryleigh. Do you want me to get Natasha or Ava's mommy to help you?"

Tears welled in her eyes, and she shook her head. "No. I'm almost four. They'll think I'm a baby." She sniffed.

"You're not a baby, Ryleigh. But you're stuck right now, right? You don't know what to do?"

She nodded and hiccupped. "I'm the stuckest, Mr. Tigger-man." Her woeful assessment made me want to fix every problem she ever had.

"It's okay to ask for help, sweetheart. Just tell me who to get."

She blinked at me. "Can you help me? Please?"

My heart cracked at her earnest plea. "I can't go in there with you. Let me call your mommy, okay?

"Okay."

I pulled out my phone and video-dialed Kami, hoping she was in a place that had good enough reception.

"Hello? Trask?"

"Hey." Her picture was dark. "Are you driving?"

"Yeah. Is everything all right?"

"Well …" I turned the camera to Ryleigh.

"Mommy, I went number two! On the train!" She giggled. "And I need help to make my poopy bum clean."

I took the phone back. "I'm not sure if I'm the one for this job, but Ryleigh is insisting. And, um, she's not wearing any clothes."

Kami chuckled. "She's three. It's common for three-year-olds to poop naked."

"Really?" That was news to me.

"Really. You have the tote bag?"

"Yes."

"Inside is a pack of flushable wipes. Hand them to Ryleigh. Ryleigh, baby, you can do this. Just wipe until there's no more poopy on the wipey, okay?"

"Okay, Mommy! I can do this 'cause I'm a big girl!"

"Yes, you are!"

I dug out the wipes and handed her one at a time, with the phone facing out. I felt incredibly awkward and was glad I didn't have to actually do the wiping part.

"I did it!" Ryleigh giggled. "All by myself. And I put all the wipes the trash!"

"Good job, baby. Now ask Mr. Trask for some clean undies and jammies 'cause I'm sure that floor is super dirty."

"No!" Ryleigh shook her head violently. "If I change, my friends will say I had an accident!"

"But sweetie, that floor is so dirty."

"But I didn't put my clothes on the floor. I hungded them on the door hook, like I do at home. Please, Mommy. I can have a bath when I get home. Please?"

Kami sighed. "Okay. But just this once. And you need to put on clean undies. Mr. Trask will find them in Mommy's bag, okay?"

"Okay!"

While Ryleigh dressed herself, I switched the call from video to audio. "Are you on your way home?" I asked Kami.

"Not yet. It'll be a late night. I have one more stop, but it's halfway to Denver."

"Okay. I'll call you when I get Ryleigh home."

"Thank you. And Trask?"

"Yeah?"

"Thank you for … everything today. I wish I could have taken her, but I'm glad you did."

"It was fun." Watching Ryleigh play with elves and run up to see Santa brought back my own happy childhood memories. "We had a great time."

"I'm so glad." Her voice broke, and she sniffed. "Thank you for being there for her."

"It was my pleasure, really."

"I love it when you say that."

I made a mental a note to say it more often.

The door squeaked open, and Ryleigh came out with a handful of wadded cloth in her extended hand. "I'll make it a point to say it more often. She's out, so I'm gonna take her back to our seat."

We hung up, and I crouched to open the tote so Ryleigh could shove her dirty undies inside.

"Did you wash your hands?" I asked gently.

Her eyes widened, and she ran back in. "I can't reach the soap!"

I smiled and went in to lift her up to the sink. Ten minutes later, she was asleep on my lap, mumbling about how she forgot her Christmas list but remembered to ask Santa for a puppy for Christmas.

I wondered how Kami felt about dogs.

BACK AT KAMI'S, I CARRIED A SLEEPING RYLEIGH TO THE DOOR. Brenna opened it before I reached the stoop. In the lit room behind her, I was surprised to see Brendan chilling on the sofa, and I noticed Brenna's usually carefully styled blond hair looked like what my sister Brooklyn liked to call "mermaid hair."

"What's Trotter doing here?" I asked. "Did you just finish at the barn?" I felt a pang of guilt for not helping like I said I would but quickly discarded it. I'd had the best time with Ryleigh, and the little glimpse I'd gotten into fatherhood had made me want it more, not spooked me like I was afraid it might.

She cleared her throat and glanced back at him. "He, um, had some ideas for the, ah, barn loft. Thinks it's big enough for office space, if I'm open to creative, um, construction. He was just leaving."

"Uh-huh." I stepped over the threshold and let Ryleigh's backpack slide off my shoulder and onto the floor.

"Let me take her," Brenna whispered.

"Noooooooooo." Ryleigh mumbled into my ear. "Story, Mr. Tiggerman."

I'm pretty sure the thumping in my chest was my heart growing—or exploding.

"Okay, Ry. I can stay for a story, but only if you let your Auntie Brenna get you ready for bed first."

"But I'm already *in* my jammies." She lifted her head up and yawned.

"You need a clean nightgown, sweetie," Brenna said. "C'mon, sweet girl. Let me get you washed up and ready for story time, okay?"

"Oh-kaaaay."

I transferred Ryleigh to Brenna's arms and watched them disappear into Ryleigh's room. When the door shut, I joined Brendan on the couch. "So. Creative construction, huh?"

He grinned. "Hell's yeah."

"So ... you and Brenna, then?"

He sighed and turned his head to look at Ryleigh's closed door. "She says she's not looking for a relationship. But there's something there. I know it. And she knows it, too."

"Give her time. If there's something there, she'll come around." As the words left my mouth, I realized the advice they carried applied to me, too.

I stood up as I heard the bedroom door open. "She's ready," Brenna announced. "Says she has an important job for you. Head on in while I walk Brendan out."

"Uh." Brendan stood up and rubbed the back of his neck. "I don't have my car, remember?"

She blushed. "Oh. Right." She looked at me. "Can you give him a ride back to Brewski's?"

"Sure." I was even more curious about what had transpired between the two, but Ryleigh appeared in the doorway and I promptly forgot about everything else.

As I approached her room, Ryleigh ran inside. I sat on the bed while she rummaged in her toy box.

"This!" She pulled out a crumpled sheet of paper and brought it to me. I lifted her onto my lap and looked at the drawing. "It's my list for Santa. My teacher help-ded me." Half a dozen smiley-face circles rested on two vertical lines. A horizontal line came out the side of each face where ears would be located—if she'd drawn them. Scribbles of blue, green, red, purple, yellow, and pink covered the vertical lines, while brown and yellow etching decorated the tops of the heads.

I was surprised at all the details she'd included. An adult hand had labeled each drawing. "You did a great job, Ry."

"I know." She pointed at the picture. "These are pretty dresses I want. All of them! And a puppy, but my teacher said I should tell Mommy about the puppy, not Santa. Can you mail my list to him? I forgotted to bring it to him. He said to give it to someone I trust."

I kissed the top of her head and forced back the water that stung my eyes. "Of course."

"Thank you!" She slid off my lap and ran back to the toy box, flinging out dolls and other things. She'd all but disappeared inside when she straightened up again.

She carried another piece of paper to me. "This is Mommy's list. I made-ed it for her. It's a *secret.*"

On the paper was a figure similar to the princesses but with green almost-rectangles dancing on the page like large confetti. I wasn't sure what to say, so I used the go-to my sister Marsha taught me to ask Mylee when I wanted her to explain something. "Tell me about it."

Ryleigh pointed to the figure. "This is Mommy. And this"—her little finger pointed to each of the green shapes—"is all the money Mommy needs so she doesn't have to go to work anymore."

"You don't want your mommy to work anymore?"

"It's okay that she workses when I go to school because I don't miss her. But I don't like it when she workses when I don't go to school."

"Why not? Your mommy's job is important." I turned her around to face me. "What don't you like about it?"

She looked down at the picture, and when she raised her head, her face crumpled. "I want ... I want to be with Mommy all the time. Daddy yells and—and—"

I pulled her to my chest. "It's okay, baby. You can tell me.

And what?" I swore to God if she said her father hurt her, I'd be in jail before morning.

"Carlotta—"

"Who's Carlotta?"

"Daddy's girlfriend. She ... she says mean things about Mommy!"

I let out a long breath, relieved that Ryleigh hadn't been hurt. But it wasn't okay for some woman to bad-mouth Kami.

"Have you told your daddy? Or your mommy?" I asked.

She nodded. "Carlotta said she would try to be nicer. But she's not trying very hard."

"Everything okay in here? I thought I heard crying." Brenna stood in the doorway.

I nodded. "Ryleigh was just telling me about Carlotta."

Brenna stiffened and frowned. "I'm familiar. Ryleigh, sweetie, how about that story now? I bet Mr. Trask's funny voices can make you forget about the not-nice lady."

I snorted. That was the plan. Though I was a little embarrassed that Ryleigh had told Brenna about my funny voices.

Ryleigh climbed under the covers, and I tucked her in and took my place on the floor next to her low bed. Halfway through the first story, she was asleep. I tiptoed out of the room and shut the door, my heart full.

16

KAMI

"There you go, baby. Perfect pom-pom hair!" I lifted Ryleigh to stand on the stool so she could see the transformation. It was a big day for her. Her mini cheer team would be performing at the Christmas at the Plex event. Held annually on the first Saturday of December, it was a fundraiser for multiple programs the sportsplex sponsored and a fun family event. Too bad her dad was "busy with work."

"I'm *so* pretty, Mommy. My face is like Auntie Chelsea's at the hockey game!" I grinned as she stared at herself and chattered on about growing up to be a spirit squad member and cheer coach. Her sparkly uniform was accented by a red flare skirt trimmed in faux fur. I'd twisted her hair into space buns and wrapped banana-curled hairpieces around them. Two bedazzled red bows and way too much makeup for an almost-four-year-old completed the look. Tentatively, she pulled at one of the curls and then giggled when she let go and it sprang back into place.

This was worth every extra hour I worked at Brewski's.

"Is it time to go now?"

"Yes, baby. Are you ready?"

"I was born ready!" she announced, flourishing her arms in the air. I snorted and helped her down from the vanity stool. "Is Daddy coming to see me?"

She'd asked every day since she'd known about the event. And every day I gave her the same reply: "If he gets out of work in time, yes."

"Is Mr. Tiggerman coming?"

Her innocent question hit me straight in the gut. It was clear how important Trask was to her—and to me—and it scared me to a point I didn't want to admit, even to myself. Because if Ryleigh and I didn't leave first—in May, after I graduated—Trask would leave us for a different team. There was a likelihood that could happen anytime, even before May. What then? Two men in Ryleigh's life would have let her down. But there was something really special about Trask, and anyone who gave so much of themselves to a kid who wasn't biologically or legally theirs.

I gave her a squeeze. "You know he'll be there. All of the Voltage players will be there, remember? They'll be skating after all the performances."

"And we're gonna take pictures and sign autographs! Like Thinter Bale does at the big park!"

"The *players* will be signing autographs. You get to take your picture with whichever ones you want after we go ice skating with them, okay?"

"Okay. But I'm going to sign, too."

There was no arguing with her.

I dropped Ryleigh off with her coaches, Amelia and Nate; waved to Chelsea, who was running the event; and then headed for the basketball gym, where the teams would be performing in about an hour's time.

"Kami!" I turned at the familiar voice shouting my name as I scanned the crowd for the faces. Chelsea's sister, Taylor, waved from the bleachers. She was engaged to Brenna's cousin Kingston, who played for Montana's NHL team. Brenna was planning their weddings, and I'd been asked to be in both of them.

I waved back and hurried up the steps to hug her. "I didn't know you'd be here!" I hugged her. "How's Montana?" I peeked around them and noticed five-year-old twins Klara and Kord sitting with a pretty blonde. "Are Kingston and Alexei here, too?"

She nodded. "In Denver. They're playing the Edge tonight." The Denver Edge was the NHL team affiliated with the Voltage. Trask had played a few games with them. "This is Alexei's sister, Petra. We took the kids this weekend to give Ginny some rest time."

"Awesome." I waved to the twins. Ginny was their aunt and had been caring for them since their parents had died in a car crash almost three years ago. Now Ginny and her husband, Alexei, were expecting their first baby.

"We came to see Ryleigh!" Klara said, pushing her way past Taylor to get to me. She lifted up a purple painted wooden clothespin. "I made this for her."

I took the clothespin and examined it. "You rock" was barely legible going down one side in silver marker. The other side had a silver sparkle overlay and said "Kali."

"That's very sweet of you, Klara," I said. "Thank you."

"It's for her backpack. I have a whole collection!" She grinned and yanked my hand down to point to the writing.

"Kali is my new team. In Montana. Kali Allstars. At competitions, you trade with friends. It's fun!"

Brenna arrived, and I chatted with her, Taylor, and Petra while we waited for the event to start. Taylor wanted to know how Nate, her former cheer partner, liked coaching the preschool team, which she'd coached until she'd moved to Montana. I told her he was loving it and the little girls got a kick out of being lifted up into the air to stand on his hands.

"Ladies and gentlemen!" We turned our attention to the floor mats, where the gym manager stood with a microphone. He explained to the audience how to assemble in front of the mats when their teams performed. I had figured we'd be watching from our seats and must have looked as confused as I felt.

"Just follow us," Taylor whispered.

He finished his announcements and introduced one of the Plex's Worlds teams, which would open the exhibition. Taylor led our group to the holding area, and I almost tripped watching the athletes fly into the air like Cirque performers. After thunderous applause and a standing ovation, we moved into place to watch the Tiny team. Klara and Kord pushed their way to the front and knelt on the edge of the mat.

"Hey." A hum of energy pulsed through me at the sound of Trask's deep voice, and I turned to greet him. My mouth dropped as over a dozen of his teammates filled into the space behind us.

"You brought the entire team?" I mentally counted—nineteen in total.

He shrugged. "Most of them. We were already here, so I bribed them with beer." He winked. "Plus, Noel has the hots for one of the girls on the team that just performed."

"I do not!" The petulant hiss from the kid standing behind Trask made me laugh. "We're just friends."

Trask raised a brow. "Whatever you say, Santa."

I chuckled at the mention of Noel's nickname. I'd heard him complaining about it on more than one occasion at Brewski's.

We turned back to the mat when the emcee announced Ryleigh's team. "Our next team is the Lil' Chargers, who will compete in the Tiny Novice division. Comprised of three- to five-year-olds, most of these athletes are new to the sport. They've been working *very* hard to learn their beginning tumbling skills and performance expressions. Please join me in welcoming to the mat the Lil' Chargers!"

My hand flew to my mouth as Ryleigh and her team jogged onto the mat from the backstage area. She was arm-in-arm with a little boy, and they almost tripped getting to their spots. I quickly pulled out my phone to record.

"You got this, Ryleigh!"

"Go, Ryleigh!"

"Get it, girl!"

Her uncertain expression turned to sheer confidence, then sass as Trask and his teammates cheered my little girl on. It was the most adorable thing I'd ever seen. Trask wasn't just winning my heart, but Ryleigh's too. My hand shook a little as I held up my phone to record the performance.

"Let me get that so you can watch." Trask's warm breath in my ear and his thoughtful suggestion, on top of him being there, was making me all gooey inside. I briefly closed my eyes and took a deep breath, pushing aside all my fears. Trask was such a good man.

Wordlessly, I passed my phone and mouthed the words "thank you" as one of the little girls called "Set!"

The athletes posed with their partners in their beginning positions. Ryleigh crossed her arms and leaned back-to-back with the little boy. As Shakira's "Try Everything" blared, they fell to the ground into forward rolls.

Ryleigh sassed her way through the routine, nodding her head, shaking her booty, and stretching her face into over-the-top expressions. I laughed and clapped along, yelling for my girl and so proud of how far she'd come in her tumbling and dancing ability in just a couple of months.

"Give it up for our Lil' Chargers!" The emcee returned to the mat as the noise reached deafening proportions. The team ran off stage, and we moved with the crowd back to the bleachers.

"Thanks so much for coming," I said to Trask.

"It was our pleasure. I've got to get back to the rink. We'll see you at the skate later?"

"We'll be there." I lifted my arms, then let them fall. I wanted to hug him, but … He must have sensed my hesitation, because his eyes lit up and he pulled me to him in a giant bear hug. My entire body tingled, and my heart shifted. Impulsively, I wound my arms around his polyester warm-up jacket and squeezed.

"I'm counting on it," he whispered into my hair.

I was, too. Now that my arms knew what he felt like, they wanted more.

I wanted more.

I was sure of that now.

17

TRASK

*T*he burn of Kami's hug didn't dissipate as I entered the cool ice arena. I'd made up my mind to ask her out tonight. If she friend-zoned me, I'd take it. I just wanted to spend more time with her—and make it abundantly clear I was interested.

I was a few minutes late for the skating event. The Flying Stars were a team of kids that the Plex sponsored. The athletes had varying disabilities, some physical, some mental. We had a warm-up session with them now, before the public event. Several wouldn't be attending the open skate due to reasons related to their condition.

Each of the Voltage players were partnered up with a buddy. My buddy was Susie Jefferson. She was seven years old and could skate circles around me, despite losing one of her legs to cancer when she was a baby.

She spotted me the second I stepped onto the ice. "Trask! I got a new leg! See?" Susie kicked her left leg out in front of her as she skated over to me. Grabbing onto my arm, she lifted her pant leg to show me her prosthetic. "Now I won't wobble so much when I walk!"

"It's nice," I replied, swallowing the lump in my throat. This girl had been through more in her short life than anyone should have to experience in a lifetime. My mother had that kind of strength, too.

"It's *very* nice," she corrected. "Let's skate fast today, okay?"

I held out my hand. "You might have to pull me along. I'm feeling kind of slow."

She rolled her eyes. "Oh, puh-lease. It's your job to skate fast. Let's go!"

With a yank of strength that challenged my balance, Susie and I were off to skate laps. She chatted the whole time and didn't stumble once.

"Your laces are loose," I observed. We slowed to a stop on the side and I bent down to retie her boot.

"Thanks!"

"You're welcome. Hey, Suz, will you be here later for the public skate?"

"Oh yeah. My family is going to be here till the fireworks!"

"That's great," I said. "I have someone I'd like you to meet."

She leaned her head closer to mine. "Oooh, is it a girlfriend?"

"No," I said too quickly. Although I liked the sound of calling Kami my girlfriend, it had been a long time since I thought of anyone in that way. I hadn't wanted to invest in anyone who didn't want to invest in me. "Just a friend and her little girl. I don't think Ryleigh—the little girl; she's only three —has skated before, and I thought you could give her some pointers."

"Oh! Yes, of course!"

"Cool." I tapped her skate. "All set."

When the session was over, I dropped her off with her parents in the lobby. I grabbed a couple of slices of pizza from the concession stand and debated waiting around or heading back to the basketball gym. That would make it obvious I was waiting for Kami, though. I didn't want to spook her.

Susie and I waited by the benches near the skate rental for Kami and Ryleigh. "There they are," I pointed to the automatic doors. "Pink coats." Both were bundled up in puffy pink jackets.

Kami and her mini-me. It surprised me when I found myself getting choked up.

"I'm on it!" Susie, skates on and all, rushed up to them and began talking emphatically with her hands and pointing to her feet. Kami glanced up, and I waved. She raised a brow and bent down to talk to the girls. Susie took Ryleigh's hand and led her to the counter, presumably to get her skates.

As Kami approached, I could feel my smile getting wider.

"Are you sure about this? Susie told me she has a prosthetic?"

"One hundred percent. Ryleigh's in good hands. Do you know Ginny Kriz?"

She nodded. "Alexei's wife? She was an Olympic skater, right?"

"She was. Susie took private lessons with her before Alexei got traded to Montana. She wants to be a paralympian."

"Wow, that's amazing. Are her parents here? I'd like to meet them."

"They're in the bleachers. Susie says they make her nervous if they're on the ice with her. They're a little overprotective."

"Can't blame them." She turned back towards the counter as the girls headed over. Susie held Ryleigh's hand and her skates.

"Mr. Tiggerman! Susie is going to teach me, so you don't have to. Right, Susie?"

"Right." She grinned and handed the skates to me. "You can teach her mom." She gave me an overexaggerated wink.

I snorted and knelt down in front of Ryleigh. "Looks like you need to get some skates, too, Kami."

Kami frowned. "I was planning to watch. I'm soooo bad. I think you hockey players would call me a bender?"

I chuckled as I slid Ryleigh's foot into a skate and pictured Kami trying to skate with her ankles bent. "I'm sure you're not that bad."

"Southern girl, remember?" *How could I forget?*

I looked up at Kami. "I got you."

Our eyes locked for a second before she nodded and walked away to get her skates. I exhaled a long breath. "All right, Ry. Let me help you stand up."

She slid off the bench and leaned from one foot to the next, her face screwing up into a pinch. "These feel funny."

"You'll get used to it, Ryleigh," Susie said. "Trask, can you carry her onto the ice? I can take it from there."

I saluted her. "Yes, ma'am." The girls giggled. I lifted Ryleigh into my arms, and when Kami returned, the four of us went inside the rink.

Kami wasn't kidding when she said she was a bender.

Keeping her from falling was a full workout, but I didn't mind. Any excuse to hold her worked for me.

"Oh, come on, Ms. Kami, you can't be that bad." Susie and Ryleigh, skating hand in hand, fell in line next to us. Susie gave me another exaggerated wink.

"I promise you, I am doing my best," Kami replied.

"Suuuuuure you are." Susie laughed.

Kami frowned as they skated off.

I laughed. "Now I'm wondering if you're really this bad."

"Guess you'll never know." She shot me a wink and grinned.

I squeezed her hand. "Maybe I don't want to."

"I can't believe Ryleigh picked this up so fast."

"She's a natural. Time for lessons?"

Kami grimaced. "Maybe when cheer season is over."

Hand in hand, we stayed behind the girls and talked about the most random things. I felt the tension leave her body a little with each lap, and we discovered we both had a passion for mystery novels, action-adventure movies, and homemade alfredo sauce.

"Do you make your own sauce?" I asked.

"I do. I'm making it tomorrow night, actually." She smiled shyly. "Maybe … maybe you'd like to join us for dinner?"

"I definitely would." Was she asking me on a date? I didn't usually eat such rich food during the season, but I wouldn't pass up an offer to spend time with her. Even if it was a friends thing and Ryleigh was there.

She blushed and looked down, which threw off her balance. "Whoa!" Her free arm flailed wildly, but I moved in front of her before she could fall, wrapping my arm around her waist.

Kami leaned into me, and suddenly it was a thousand degrees in the rink. "Thank you." Her face was so close to mine, I could feel the warm puff of breath that left her mouth. Pepperminty.

I gulped back a lump and steadied her in front of me. "You're welcome."

A whistle blew, a signal to us to keep moving. I held her hand tightly, more from not wanting to let go than for physical support.

She might have been the one unsteady on her feet, but it was me that was falling hard and fast.

18

KAMI

*W*atching Trask monitor Susie teaching Ryleigh to skate kept my heart in a steady rhythm of happy beats. Ryleigh hadn't wanted to use the skate trainer, so at the beginning, Trask kept her upright while Susie instructed. Within minutes, they were off skating on their own.

We skated behind them, hand in hand. He kept me upright every time I wobbled. It wasn't hard for me to imagine what it might be like being in a relationship with him. I had no doubt he'd jump to support me wherever else I might falter. I was grateful for our new friendship and the attention he gave my girl, and I didn't want to lose what we'd built. He genuinely seemed to like spending time with Ryleigh and other kids. His teammates did, too. Around us, every one of them was hand in hand with one or two kids. They were all starting to feel like family. I was thrilled Trask had accepted my invitation to dinner tomorrow. Although, going out to a restaurant with him—alone—sounded nice too.

The session ended, and we made our way to the benches to take our skates off. Trask carried Ryleigh off the ice, a beaming Susie at his side.

"Mommy! That was so fun!" I took her from him and plunked her down on the bench next to me. "When can we do it again?"

I looked up at Trask, who smiled and shrugged. "I guess anytime Mr. Trask is available."

"You mean Mr. Tiggerman!" Susie shouted, and the girls collapsed into a giggling fit.

Trask just shook his head. I loved that he had a sense of humor about Ryleigh's ridiculous nicknames.

Susie's mom came over to collect her, and the girls hugged goodbye. I was glad Ryleigh had made a new friend today.

"What are you ladies planning next?" Trask asked.

"I'm not sure. Ryleigh, are you hungry?" We'd eaten dinner in the gym, but Ryleigh was usually ready for a snack after physical activity.

"No. Yes! Can we get hot chocolate and thestnuts?"

"Thestnuts? Do you mean chestnuts?" I was used to her lispy pronunciations, but sometimes they threw me.

"Yeah. Thestnuts. In a bag. And can we go in the sleigh?"

"We can try. There might be a long line, though."

"It's okay. Mr. Tiggerman, can you come with us?"

"I have to do the meet and greet now. But I'm sure I can reserve a time later, if that's okay?"

I nodded, and we went to the craft fair to pass the time. We ran into Svetlana, Dmitri, and Natasha, and they invited us to go with the team the next day to pick out a Christmas tree at a nearby farm. I'd just been planning to get a small artificial one, but Ryleigh was so excited, I couldn't say no.

An hour later, we met up with Trask, and bundled up under a fur blanket, the three of us coasted in a sleigh around the back fields of the Plex. I was completely content and enjoying every moment with my girl. And now, snuggled up with her and an amazing guy that liked us a lot, I couldn't help but think that this is what it *should* feel like at Christmastime.

The crisp air nipped at my face, but under the blanket, I was toasty. I leaned into Trask's side, telling myself it was for the added warmth, but even I couldn't make myself believe that lie. His arm rested behind us, and I seemed to nestle perfectly to him. Bright stars sparkled above us in the clear night sky, and I lost myself in the romance of the moment.

"I think she's sleeping," Trask leaned over to whisper.

I bent to check the still form that leaned against my side. "I think you're right."

"She's an amazing kid," Trask said. "You're doing a wonderful job raising her."

"Thank you." His compliment had me all choked up. "I really am trying to do the best I can."

"I know you are. And it's good to see you having fun instead of just working."

"It's good to be having fun." I snuck a glance at him and flushed when I caught him staring at me. Our eyes locked as the moonlight lit up his face.

"Are you … available next week? For fun?"

My heartbeat sped up. Was he asking me on a date? "Um …" I glanced at Ryleigh.

"Just you, Kami."

"Just me? Like … a date? Or as friends?"

He studied me. I blinked. I didn't want this to be awkward. A date might end in a kiss. Was I ready for that?

I think I wanted to be.

That was terrifying.

There were so many reasons why I shouldn't date Trask, the biggest of which being I was moving home next summer, and who knew where his career would take him? Ryleigh was already getting so close to him. If we tried dating, what would that do to her?

"What do you think?" he finally answered. I held my breath, debating between what I should say and what I wanted to say.

"I'm not sure I can do anything more than friends right now," I said hurriedly, a sense of panic coming out of nowhere. A shadow crossed his face. I hated to disappoint him—and myself. "Ryleigh's dad has her Thursday after school until Sunday sometime."

"Thursday, then. I'm leaving Friday morning for a few away games."

"Sounds great. I have that night off work, too." I broke eye contact and turned to face forward. It felt like I'd been in some sort of dream state. When our eyes connected, I'd had tunnel vision. Everything around me blurred and fell away. I'd never experienced a connection like that. It was otherworldly.

I needed to change the subject. "Are you going to the Christmas tree farm tomorrow?" I asked.

"I wasn't planning on it. Jason said he was going, and we don't need two trees. Why do you ask?"

"Svetlana invited me. It sounds fun. I've never been to one."

"Me neither, actually. Not really a South Carolina thing."

"Nope!" I smiled. "But… Maybe…you'd want to go with us

and help Ryleigh and I pick out a tree?" He probably thought I was nuts, being so hot and cold in the same conversation. I was still working through some things, but I was determined to knock down my own walls.

"It would be my pleasure."

I laughed. "Of course it would. So we'll see you tomorrow, then?"

"Definitely."

THE PALMER CITY CHRISTMAS TREE FARM WAS ON THE western edge of town. Trask picked us up in his truck, and after only a few minutes of struggling and grunting—with Ryleigh cheering us on—we managed to secure her car seat in the extended cab.

The Antonovs, Wards, and other members from the team gathered in the parking lot, awaiting the arrival of everyone else. I loved that about this group—they were a team in every sense of the word. Some were only here for a season or less, but while they were a Volt, they were tight. Once a Volt, always a Volt, Trask had told me.

Coach Conway arrived last, with Noel Allaire and his mother, Gemma. I'd met her a few times, and we'd chatted about mom stuff. Noel seemed close to his mother and didn't seem to mind that she was involved with the team. She and the coach had become good friends, and some of the younger players had even taken to calling her "Mom."

We checked in at the main building, and the guys were given handsaws and rope. As we turned down the first path of trees, Ryleigh broke free from my hand to run up at the front with the other children.

I smiled at Trask when I caught him stealing a glance at me. "Thanks for bringing us here today." I adjusted my scarf nervously. "Ryleigh said she's not going to leave until she's sure she finds the prettiest tree. Are you prepared to be here a while?"

He laughed. "As long as it takes."

"You're a champ," I said. "She's very fickle."

"I disagree. She seems to know exactly what she wants." He was right, of course. How well he knew my daughter sent a flutter swirling around in my belly. Ryleigh always knew what she wanted, unlike me, who second-guessed just about every decision I made.

We walked farther, and Jason and Lauren fell into step with us as others found their trees and veered off the main path.

"Have you decided where you're going to put your tree?" Trask asked.

"It depends how big it is." Yesterday, when we chatted about the tree farm, I'd explained I wasn't sure where I'd put a large tree. Last year, I'd purchased a three-foot synthetic for the front window ledge, and it had been enough since we'd gone home for Christmas. The cottage was so small, there were only a couple of spots that would fit it if we rearranged some things.

Ryleigh turned around on the path. "We need a BIG tree, Mommy! Daddy has a big tree at my other house. Please, Mommy!"

Her plea ripped at my heart. I swallowed and nodded.

"Whatever you choose, baby girl. We'll find a way to make it fit."

"Oh goody!" She looked back as Natasha and her family turned off the path and stopped at a large spruce. "These trees are too prickly. Let's keep walking!"

We trudged on. "Here!" Ryleigh called, and we turned off the main path among a path of grand firs. She stopped after a few trees and pointed to a short, round one. "This is my tree! Look how big around it is! Cut it down, boys!"

I snorted as Trask and Jason set to work cutting the tree. Ryleigh supervised as Lauren and I looked on.

"She's an amazing little girl, Kami. I love her personality." Lauren watched the scene before us with pure delight on her face.

"Thank you," I said. "Do you miss teaching the littles?" She'd recently had to switch from teaching first grade to fourth grade.

"I do. It's easy to fix their problems and comfort them when they're little. They just need love. The older kids … they don't believe in magic, you know? They're too cynical, and there are so many academic and societal pressures. It's hard to be a kid these days."

I nodded, unsure of what to say. "I'm savoring every moment like this. I know it will all go really fast."

"Okay, Ryleigh," Trask called. "Yell 'timber' so it will fall!"

"Tim-berrrrrrrrrrrrrrrrrr!" She giggled as the guys slowly let the tree fall to the ground.

Ten minutes later, she'd chosen a tree for Jason and Trask's apartment, and we were on our way back to the main building for tree netting and hot chocolate with the team.

When Ryleigh, Natasha, and Ava started to argue over which of their trees was better, Kira, Svetlana, and I determined it was time to go. Ryleigh chatted the entire way home, explaining to us why the grand fir was better than the Colorado spruce and the white pine. Apparently, softer needles were the most important quality in a tree, then color, and then "empty space for ornaments." Not for the first time, I didn't mind that her current preschool was pricier than the last one.

Back at our house, I settled Ryleigh at the table with the coloring book the tree farm had sent us home with. While Trask prepped and set up the tree next to the fireplace, I started dinner. I loved to cook, and Ryleigh was a good eater, as far as preschoolers went. She loved most vegetables and would try new foods without a fight.

Trask joined Ryleigh at the table as I turned the burner off under the pan of chicken. "The prettiest tree in the land is ready for lights and ornaments!" he announced with a grin.

Ryleigh clapped. "Yay! Can we decorate now, Mommy?"

"I think we're supposed to let it sit for a day." I glanced at Trask for confirmation.

"But…" She stared at it forlornly. "You said I have to go to Daddy's tomorrow. I want to decorate it today." Her voice wavered, and she sniffed. I pressed my lips together and looked at the tree, debating. "What do you think, Trask?"

He shrugged. "It's dry, critter-free, and not too sappy. I think it's okay."

Ryleigh squealed and jumped from her seat. "I'm going to go get all my dollies!"

We watched her go and shared a laugh. When our eyes met, we held each other's gaze. I sucked in a breath as I read the heat in his eyes. This man seemed to be everything I could want, and it scared the heck out of me.

"Do you need any help getting anything from your attic? I assume you have an attic?" He broke the silence, and I let go of the breath I'd been holding.

"We do." I cleared my throat. I turned away to drain the pasta. "There's a pull-down staircase in the laundry room. The Christmas bins are clear and have red covers."

"On it."

I finished prepping the dinner alone in the kitchen, feeling both of their absences. Ryleigh was in and out of her room, carrying a few dolls with each trip and then lining them up in a row on the sofa. Trask brought the bins down and stacked them by the wall. I took another deep breath as I thought about all the memories those totes held. I wanted to make new memories to record over the unpleasant ones. Sutton and I had fought every Christmas, each year about a different minor detail that never really mattered but only ever ate at our connection. After Ryleigh's second Christmas, I'd had enough, and as I put away the decorations that year, I knew it was time for us to go our separate ways.

I didn't want to open those totes.

I portioned out the pasta, chicken, broccoli, and alfredo sauce. As good of an eater as she was, Ryleigh did not like her food touching, and I'd gotten used to keeping it separated.

I felt Trask behind me before I saw him. "Sure I can't help?" I closed my eyes. His voice in my ear and warm breath on my neck sent thrills through me. And he smelled like a Christmas tree.

"I've got it." My reply sounded husky, and I wondered if he knew the effect he was having on me. I stared down at the plates. They looked like pie graphs. A ramekin of sauce sat in each center, noodles on one side, and chicken and broccoli—not touching—on the other half. "Unless you prefer your foods mixed?"

He laughed. "I'm guessing this is a Ryleigh thing?" I nodded. He picked up the three plates expertly and waggled his eyebrows. "I'll let Ryleigh lead on this one."

I just about melted on the spot. My girl seemed to have him wrapped around her finger, and he was aware and liking it.

I picked up the basket of crescent rolls and turned around. Trask was staring at the tree. I followed his gaze. "What the—" Standing frozen in place, I stared at the tree. "Ryleigh, honey, what *are* you doing?"

"I'm making my tree SUPER pretty, Mommy!" she announced gleefully. "Mr. Tiggerman, can you put me up high so I can make the top pretty, too?"

In a matter of a few minutes, Ryleigh had stuck almost all of her princess dolls into the tree.

"Sap," I whispered, hoping this farm tree wouldn't leave any sticky residue in the dolls' hair. I cleared my throat. "What about the ornaments?"

"Ornaminths are boring," she stated emphatically, rolling her eyes. "I told you we were going to have the prettiest tree. Pretty trees need pretty dresses. Mr. Tiggerman! Up, please!"

Trask set the plates on the table and tried to reassure me. "It's not that sappy." His lips twitched, but the cost of her two-dozen-plus dolls and the chore of getting sap out of dolly ball gowns had me cringing.

Ryleigh took him by the hand and dragged him over to the

sofa, where she gathered the remaining dolls in her arms. "Up now, please!"

I nodded, and he obeyed Ryleigh's request, lifting her up so she could stuff the dolls into the upper branches. "We just need the angel now. Mommy, can you get the angel?"

The angel. I sucked in a breath. I'd left that at the old house on purpose. Sutton and I had bought it for our first Christmas together. "It's not here, baby girl. I left it at your daddy's."

She shook her head, frowning. "It's not. He has a new one."

"How about a star?" Trask suggested. *Bless him.* "A big yellow one. I could help you make it."

"Oooh, I know!" Ryleigh shook her head and scrambled down from his shoulder. She ran from the room and was back in seconds with a glittery yellow princess wand. The star at the tip lit up when the user slid a switch.

"Perfect." Trask lifted her to the top of the tree, and she slid it into place.

Yes. Perfect.

After dinner, I thanked Trask again for a wonderful day. "You were a good sport, letting her boss you around," I joked as we sat on the couch with hot chocolate, watching Ryleigh set up a collection of plastic character figurines under the tree in her own version of the Nativity scene.

"She's so smart, knows what she wants, and isn't afraid to buck tradition. I admire that."

"Same. I never thought there was so much to learn from a three-year-old."

"My sister says Mylee teaches her more about life than the other way around. It must be amazing to be a parent. I mean, look at her." At the tree, Ryleigh was now acting out the birth of baby Jesus with Ariel, Erik, and a baby version of Moana.

"You made her, Kami. You grew a human being inside you, and now she's her own person. It's pretty incredible."

It *was* pretty incredible. And for him to notice and articulate it and not be afraid to say it out loud ... *he* was pretty incredible.

19

TRASK

hursday night, I pulled up in front of Kami's house five minutes early. Even though it wasn't an official date, I was nervous. I hadn't been on many official-type dates, having had long-term girlfriends in high school and college. Both had broken up with me when I left, and after the big college breakup, I made a promise to myself not to get into a relationship until I had a standard contract with the NHL.

I wasn't going to get my heart broken again. It took a toll on my playing and my mental health. But Kami...

I didn't think Kami was the sort to use a guy for his status and dump him when his popularity could no longer serve her, like my exes did, but she had a little girl. If I got attached—or worse, if Ryleigh got too attached to me—and I had to leave, I'd feel awful. Better to nurture the friendship, and then maybe someday when we were both back in South Carolina, if it was meant to be, it would happen.

Before I could reach the house, the door opened and Kami appeared. I stopped halfway up the walk and just stared. Even bundled up, she was beautiful. Under her knit hat, her brown hair fell in waves down the front of her short jacket. Fitted jeans hugged her hips and disappeared into brown boots just below her knee.

She was perfect.

"Hey." Her breath puffed in the air as she hurried toward me.

"Hi." My hands fidgeted in my pockets.

Kami slid her arm under mine and turned me toward the street. "I still can't believe you haven't been to Papa Raffino's. It's the best pizza in town!"

"I keep meaning to. But it's hard not to keep going back to Brewski's. The service there is the best."

Kami chuckled, and we chatted lightly as we walked around the block toward Main Street. She'd made a reservation, so we were seated right away. The traditional Italian eatery had low lighting, wooden booths, and murals of vineyards painted on the side walls.

"So, what's your favorite pizza?" I asked, scanning the extensive menu. "I'll eat anything except anchovies."

She made a face. "No worries there. I like the South Shore bar pizza, though."

"What's that?"

"It's a pan-style pizza with a biscuity kind of crust and mostly cheddar cheese. The sauce and cheese go all the way to edge of the pan, making it a greasy, crispy, buttery mess. And it's *especially* delicious with pineapple and ham."

I stared at her, trying to process what I'd heard. "Pineapple on a pizza? With ham? How did they even come up with that?"

"The best!" She laughed. "The owners' daughter-in-law is from the Boston area. It's a staple there. When she moved here last year, she missed it so much, they added it to the menu."

"Okay, I guess I'll try it. You want to share a large pizza then?"

"No can do. Bar pizza is personal-size only. You up for taking a risk?"

I grinned and leaned back in the booth. "I'm usually up for trying new things. And I do love challenges." And maybe I wanted to impress Kami a bit.

Okay, I wanted to impress Kami *a lot*.

She smiled back. "We'll see."

The pizza was so good, I ate all of it and a quarter of Kami's. I could tell she was pleased.

I reached for the bill when it came, but she laid her hand on top of mine to stop me. The warmth of her hand on mine sent a jolt of awareness sizzling through me.

"I'm really glad you liked it. Let me treat you?" she asked.

I stared at her hand, still on mine and sending sparks up my arm. Such a simple gesture, but it was having a complicated effect on me. I took a steadying breath before I spoke. "Thank you. Let me get dessert then? Maybe we can stop at that crepes place we passed a few buildings down?"

"I'd love that. And it's not that cold—we could bring them to the park. There's a bench by the Christmas tree that's a great spot at night. The colored lights reflect off the snow, and it looks like a magical wonderland."

"Sounds perfect." And romantic. Maybe she'd change her mind about the friends thing.

Outside, Kami tucked her arm through mine again. We strolled lazily, breathing in the crisp, pine-scented air and taking in the holiday decorations and comparing them to outdoor décor back home. Garland-wrapped lampposts, connected by strings of colored lights, lit our pathway to Crepe Suzette's, a stark contrast to the twinkle-light-wrapped sabal palms in our Lowcountry neighborhoods.

Soft tunes from the 1940s played from outdoor speakers along our route, and I felt like I was on the set of an old Christmas movie. I loved having her on my arm and felt the absence of her closeness when we got our crepes. The bistro folded them in a triangle for easy handling on the go.

"Try it before it gets cold," Kami urged.

I bit into the warm treat, savoring the fruit inside. "Wow, that's amazing."

"It's my favorite." She opted for whipped cream on hers, and when she took a bite, it left a puffy white mustache under her nose. I wanted to kiss it off more than I wanted to win our next game.

"Shoot, we forgot napkins," she said, stretching her tongue up to swipe the whipped cream.

I held back a groan as a flood of inappropriate thoughts rushed through my mind. "You missed some. May I?"

She nodded, and I gently wiped the corner of her mouth. Her full lips were bare and cold, and she shivered despite the warm crepe. It took every ounce of strength I had not to lean down and warm them up with my own.

"Thanks." She pressed her lips together, and I just continued to stare at her mouth. "You're staring," she whispered.

"Sorry. I—I can't help it."

Our eyes locked, and we didn't need words to communicate what we were both feeling. It was clear she felt the chemistry between us. Was she weighing the risk as I was?

Her hand dropped, and she laced her arm through mine again. "Let's go to the park."

We crossed over the creek bridge just south of the park. The soft swishing sound of the water flowing over the rocks was soon replaced by the Christmas music projecting from hidden speakers.

"This way." Kami wove us through the trees toward the massive pine at the northern end. I'd driven by it countless times but never stopped to appreciate it. "Oh good, it's empty."

Ahead of us, just to the right of the tree, a wrought-iron bench sat in the warm glow of the lights. Kami let out a happy sigh as we sank down onto it. I wondered if she'd even noticed it was as cold as an ice bath. Our thighs touched, and again my pulse kicked up a notch. I slid away just enough so that we weren't touching. The cool absence of the heat from her leg through our jeans calmed me.

We finished our crepes in silence, basking in the ambience. Not a moment felt awkward, and I hesitated to speak, fearing my voice would cut into the mood.

I needed a minute to think about being this close to her and staying within the friend-zone rules. I gathered our trash and walked it to the nearest bin. On the way back, I decided it wouldn't do any harm to extend my arm. When I returned, I took a risk, stretching my arm behind her to rest it on the back of the bench.

Kami leaned her head into my shoulder. "You ever just sit and wonder if you'd followed certain advice, where your life would be right now?"

"Yeah." I felt that deeply. "But I try not to dwell on it. I don't want to have any regrets, you know?"

"I have a lot of regrets." She shifted, pulling her legs up and crossing them on the bench.

"I hope you don't regret tonight." I slid my arm off the bench and cupped her shoulder.

"Just one thing about it." I turned to find her looking up at me. Again, I felt that we were talking with our eyes.

"What's that?" My breath puffed out in a cold cloud between us, blurring her features, but there was nothing blurry about what she wasn't saying. But I wanted to hear her say it.

"That friend-zone line I drew ... Do you think it would be a bad idea to cross it?"

"I don't know, but I know I want to cross it." I angled my face over hers. Our lips met, and what I thought would be a quick, gentle kiss was anything but.

Kami wrapped her arms around my neck and tugged me closer. I kissed her with everything I had. I wanted her to know—no, to feel—that this meant something to me. I needed her to know that this was important.

"Wow," she breathed, pulling away. "I've never been kissed like that before."

"That's a crime. We should kiss again so you can't say that anymore."

She grinned and climbed onto my lap. "Kiss me like that till they turn the tree lights off?"

"With pleasure."

20

KAMI

*M*y lips were swollen from too much kissing.

I take that back.

There was no such thing as too much kissing where Trask Emerson was concerned.

I said goodbye to him at the door, afraid we might get carried away if I invited him in. The house always felt empty when Ryleigh was gone, but tonight I also felt the loss of a partner. Her dad and I had been in love once. I hadn't known until tonight how much I missed that feeling of euphoria that came from connecting with someone on such a personal, heartfelt level.

Someone to keep me warm at night, wake up with in the morning. Help me get Ryleigh ready for school, spend the holidays with. Normal yet priceless things, gifts that money couldn't buy. It had been almost two years since I'd missed those things.

Trask made me miss those things.

Tonight, I'd felt alive again. He'd made me feel like I was a prize to be claimed. The mark of his kiss left an impression on my heart and lifted my spirit.

I brewed myself a cup of tea and filled the tub. I needed to relax my nerves and not overthink what tonight meant. A hot bath and a new audiobook ought to help.

I sank into the hot water. As I swiped to hit "play" for the book, a call from Brenna popped up and I accidentally swiped to answer the call.

"I saw your bathroom light on, so I know you're home!"

Shoot, I forgot I was on her way home. "Um … I was going to call you tomorrow?"

"Is that a question?"

"Maybe?"

"So how did it go?"

I closed my eyes and thought about how to answer. "It was … good."

"Just good? Is he still in the friend zone?"

"Brenna!"

"What? You haven't been kissed in almost two years. If it was me, you can bet I'd pull that gorgeous face down to mine!"

I wasn't going to tell her that had been one of my thoughts just before I instigated our first smooching session.

"Your silence confirms everything I need to know. Don't worry, I won't tell anyone."

"Um, thanks?"

She chuckled. "See you at work tomorrow. May you have sweet dreams of hunky hockey players."

"Thanks, Bren." I ended the call and queued up the audio-book. I needed to be distracted. It was a good thing he'd be away all weekend. These feelings were scaring me.

Trask was leaning up against the bar Tuesday afternoon when I came out of the kitchen. He flashed me a grin that heated my cheeks and sent a wave of fire down to my toes. Seeing him in person made me realize just how much I missed him over the past few days. I delivered my order quickly and hurried over.

"Four more days," he said in that soft, low voice that made me all shivery.

I'm sure my face turned redder. We'd be flying out Saturday morning for his sister's wedding. "I can't wait," I said honestly. "Ryleigh is excited, too."

"Is Sutton still giving you a hard time about it?"

"Surprisingly, no." I filled a glass of water for him and set it on the bar. When I'd told Sutton about our weekend plans, he hadn't been happy. But he hadn't mentioned it in a few days, so I wasn't worrying about it. "He's been super moody, though. I think he and his girlfriend are having problems."

"I'd say I was sorry, but …"

I grinned at him. "Sutton deserves every ounce of misery he gets."

Trask shook his head and reached for my hand. "Dumbest dude ever."

I stared at his hand holding mine, then let my gaze travel up his forearm to the biceps and triceps outlined by his form-fitting cable-knit sweater. The man was pure sex on a stick, effortless hotness, and he was interested in me.

"Yeah. Totally stupid."

"Yeah." He squeezed my hand. "So, um, I'm not sure what you're going to think about this …"

My eyes snapped up from ogling his sweater-clad torso. "That doesn't sound good."

"My sister *kind of* got the impression we were dating when I talked to her yesterday."

"Kind of?" I raised a brow and leaned into the bar. "Do elaborate," I teased. I felt a giddy thrill at the prospect of being more than just a plus-one at the wedding.

"Well, she was calling to confirm RSVPs, and she asked me if I'd asked you out yet. I told her we went out for pizza Friday, and she teased about it being a date, and I didn't correct her fast enough and—"

"Let me guess. Her mind *kind of* filled in the blanks and then you didn't correct her?"

The corner of his mouth turned up, but his eyes sparkled with amusement. "How'd you guess?"

"Brenna did pretty much the same thing to me Friday night."

He chuckled. "So, then ... are we dating? Because if you'd like to, I'd like to."

"That sounds like a song." I pressed my lips together as I wracked my brain for any reason dating Trask was a bad idea. The biggest reason was Ryleigh. If—more likely when—he left Palmer City for the career he deserved, and we broke up, it would devastate my girl. Was it selfish of me to deny us both happiness, though, even if it were only for a short while? We'd talked about how we both wanted to go back to South Carolina…Even if now wasn't our time, maybe at some point our roots would bring us back together.

But this was the present. And I liked him—a lot. And so did Ryleigh. And truthfully, we were both already attached. It would be dumb to sacrifice happy now for potential sadness later, right? And who's to say there would be sadness later? What if everything worked out?

Carpe diem.

"Yes," I said decisively, squeezing his hand back. "I'd like to. Our not-date that was a date? It was—"

"Amazing."

"Yeah, and it scared me a little. The kissing … it was intense."

"Because it mattered." Trask took my hand and sandwiched it between his. "It scared me a little, too. But I've learned if it doesn't scare you, it's not big enough."

21

TRASK

The rest of the week passed in a blur, and by Saturday night, I'd kissed Kami a dozen more times, sneaking kisses in the Brewski's parking lot and at her house while Ryleigh was distracted by fairy movies.

I wanted her to know that if a relationship between us didn't work out, I'd still be there for Ryleigh, whether she needed help or not. I loved spending time with Ryleigh, and she was teaching me a lot about myself in the process.

Like how fashionable sparkly fingernails were.

When we checked in to our flight, I noticed the airline employee smirking as I held out our tickets. I shrugged and grinned at her. The clear gloss with specks of metallic silver and gold didn't bother me, and it made Ryleigh happy. Kami hadn't commented on them, but I caught her looking at my hands a few times and smiling. What made her and her girl happy made me happy. I'd let Ryleigh paint my toes, too, if she wanted to.

I gestured for Kami and Ryleigh to walk ahead of me down the jetway and rolled our carry-ons like a badge of honor. It felt to me like we were a little family going on a vacation, and that thrilled me and scared me at the same time.

Kami led Ryleigh to our row at the back of the plane and settled Ryleigh in the middle seat. I opened the overhead compartment and lifted up their carry-on.

"Right behind you, Dad." A flight attendant squeezed behind me, and his words squeezed my heart. I looked down to see if Kami or Ryleigh had heard, but their heads were bent over Ryleigh's tablet.

I didn't correct him. As I stowed my own bag, I thought again how easy it would be to step into that role. Was I ready for that? I was already attached, despite trying not to put myself in that position.

Time would tell. I closed the overhead compartment and sat down. "What are we watching?"

"The Pirate Fairy!"

I caught Kami's eye, and she shrugged. "How many times have you watched this one already this week?" I asked.

Ryleigh thought for a moment. "All the times!"

I chuckled. "Here, let's slide your tablet into the seat pocket until we get up high, okay?"

"Okay. Mommy said that's a rule. There are so many rules on this plane! Did you know I can't eat peanut butter and jelly on the plane?"

I nodded seriously. "Peanut butter can make a lot of people sick."

"That's what Mommy said." She sighed. "She said people are 'lergic and can't breathe, like the old man who got bit by the bee."

Kami explained. "The last time we went home, one of

Grandpa Silly's friends got stung. We had to call the paramedics."

"I'm sorry to hear that."

"It happens every now and again on the tours. Luckily, everyone has been okay once they've been treated."

"So what's it like growing up on a bee farm?" I asked.

"Magical." She got a faraway look in her eyes. "Acres of play space among shady magnolias and all kinds of flowers. I grew up learning how to make all kinds of things from honey and wax—candles, soap, lip balm, lotion, face cream, you name it. In the summer, when my sisters and I were off from school, we helped Mama run the gift shop."

"That sounds amazing. How did that lead you to earth science?" I wanted to know everything.

"It always fascinated me, the role the soil played in growing the plants and how some plants thrived in our climate but not in others. Peaches in the South, apples up north. Mud versus marsh. I chose to go to college in Colorado so I could investigate the differences." She blushed. "You must think I'm such a nerd."

"Not at all." I wanted to reach out and hold her hand, but Ryleigh was between us. "I can't wait for a tour."

She grinned. "You got it."

The rest of the flight passed quickly, too quickly. I wanted more time alone with her before we had to meet my family.

Kami's sisters and parents were waiting for us in the parking lot when we arrived at the rehearsal. It still floored me that my sister Brooklyn had chosen the venue that belonged to the woman I was falling for. If that wasn't fate, I didn't know what was.

We followed a path around the entry building, which held

the gift shop, and into a garden where an arch had been set up. My family and the bridal party were standing in small groups near the arch, waiting for the rehearsal to start.

"Uncle Trask!"

I squatted down to catch the purple blur torpedoing toward me. "How's my girl?" I asked Mylee.

She frowned and slitted her eyes. "You always say, 'How's my *favorite* girl?' like that song you sing to me." Shifting in my arms, she pointed to Ryleigh. "Is *she* your favorite girl now?"

Yikes, when did four-year-olds get so perceptive? I angled my mouth over her ear. "You'll always be my favorite. Just don't tell Ryleigh, okay? We don't want her to be sad."

"Oh no." Mylee looked aghast. "No sadness at weddings!"

To save money, Brooklyn and Brian opted to do the rehearsal dinner barbecue-style in my older sister Marsha's backyard. After I introduced her to my parents, Kami and I sat with Marsha and her husband, Chad, watching Ryleigh and Mylee swing and slide on the massive playset.

"They're getting along great," Marsha said. "Mylee was afraid she'd be the only kid at the wedding."

"Ryleigh reminds me of Mylee so much," I said. "I knew they'd be fast friends." It hit me how easily Kami and Ryleigh were fitting in with my family. Like they were meant to be here.

"They do seem to have a lot in common," Kami remarked.

Suddenly, the girls erupted in a fit of giggles. I watched as they looked over at us, pointed and giggled some more. I waved, which caused more giggling,

They slid down the slide and ran toward us. Mylee climbed into my lap while Ryleigh went to Kami. "Uncle Trask, is it true?" she asked. "Do they call you the Tiggerman?"

Now we all were laughing. "Just Ryleigh," I said. "Why?"

"It *is* true!" Mylee's expression was beyond gleeful. "That's so funny!" She slid off my lap and ran to Marsha, already on to the next thing. "Mommy, where's my basket? I want to show Ryleigh how I practice."

"You left it at your Auntie Brooklyn's table, I think."

"Okay!"

The girls were off again, and I just sat there, sipping a drink and smiling. It was good to be home, and any thoughts of Kami feeling awkward around my family were erased the longer we sat here.

I looked up when I saw Brooklyn being pulled toward us, each of the little girls tugging a hand.

"Mylee had an idea, and I think it's wonderful," Brooklyn announced.

"I'm gonna be a flower girl!" Ryleigh jumped, pulling on Brooklyn's hand. "If you say yes, Mommy?"

"Um ..." Kami looked from Ryleigh to Brooklyn. "You don't have a flower girl dress, sweetie. I don't think there's time before the wedding tomorrow to get you one."

Ryleigh's lower lip stuck out and quivered. Brooklyn spoke quickly. "She can wear any dress she'd like."

"Can I wear my Thinter Bale dress?" Ryleigh asked. "It's soooo pretty!"

Kami covered her mouth with her hand, hiding a smile. "I'm not sure that's what Brooklyn had in mind when she said you could wear *any* dress."

"But—"

"I know!" Mylee shouted. "You can wear my first dress, Ryleigh!"

"That's right," Marsha said. "Mylee outgrew the first dress

we bought her, and I keep forgetting to return it. I'm sure it will fit you, Ryleigh."

"It's beeeeeeautiful! Come on! Let's go to my room and dress up!" She took Ryleigh's hand, and they were off again.

It was so easy to imagine Kami and Ryleigh fitting into my family. Suddenly, I wasn't scared anymore. I knew in my soul that they were my future and I'd do everything in my power to hold onto them, even when my job took me away.

22

KAMI

*A*fter I tucked Ryleigh into bed at my parents' house, I went downstairs to visit with them and my twin sisters. Kassidy and Khloe were twenty-four years old and still lived at home so they could help with the family farm and save money to fund building their own business.

With an MBA, Kassidy was the logical, brilliant brain behind the operation, and Khloe was the creative visionary. They were mirror twins, opposite in every way, from their personalities to the way they parted their hair.

"Are you sure you don't need any help tomorrow? It feels strange for me to be in the guest section basking in the fruits of your labors," I asked, curling up in my favorite recliner. I tapped my leg to signal to Rhett, our old cocker spaniel. At twelve, he was still able to scramble up onto the furniture.

"We're good!" Khloe assured me. "We're just so glad you're here and able to stay through Christmas. This Trask guy must really like you."

I buried my face in Rhett's neck so they wouldn't see me blush. I hadn't told them we were dating. I wasn't ready to answer all the questions yet. Let them all think we were just friends for now. It would be easier.

Kassidy plopped down next to Dad on the couch. "Well, I like him already. Don't you, Daddy?"

"I like that he called me Mr. Ellis and sir. Shook my hand like a man. Very respectful. Unlike that other one. Even as a kid, he acted more important than he was. Not a humble bone in his body."

None of us had a response to that, but I knew my sisters agreed with our father's assessment. It had been one of the things that had made Sutton so attractive to me—and others. He was tall, built, tough, and had confidence for days. Not quite a bad boy but oozed sex appeal. Every girl had a crush on him in high school, and he picked *me*. I'd felt special. Until he got bored. After Ryleigh was born, it was like his attraction for me died. I'd felt ugly and unwanted and found solace in caring for Ryleigh. She replaced him as my entire world, and I was sure that didn't help, either.

My mother walked into the room, phone to her ear, and held a finger up to her lips. "Well, that's wonderful, Bonnie. Y'all are welcome to spend Christmas morning with us ... No, ma'am, all my girls are busy with the wedding tomorrow, and we are sitting tight to host extended family Christmas Eve. You'll make sure Sutton understands that, won't you, dear? ... Oh yes, please do bring your breakfast biscuit casserole. We all missed that last year ... All right now. See you then. Buh-bye."

Mama ended the call, shaking her head. "Bless her heart, I don't think that woman understands what divorce means. Kami, dear, that was Bonnie Spencer calling to inform me that her son will also be joining us all Christmas morning."

I shook my head and tried to keep my voice level. I'd gath-ered as much from her end of the conversation but needed to know more. "He told me he was staying in Colorado Springs with his girlfriend for Christmas because he had to work on the twenty-sixth. Don't tell me he's bringing her? Mama, do not let that woman in this house. Ryleigh doesn't like her."

My mother sat on the couch next to Daddy and patted his knee. "I'm not sorry to say this, but apparently the woman has broken things off with him. Apparently, he got all bent out of shape and went on and on about how unpleased he was about you traveling here with 'that jock.'"

"He told his mother that?" I couldn't believe it.

"Of course not, dear. Carlotta called Bonnie hoping for a sympathetic ear and of course didn't receive it. You know how much Bonnie loves you and is hoping for a reconcilia-tion. Carlotta is smart enough to know if a man's mama doesn't like you, you stand no chance in the long run."

"I hope that doesn't mean he's planning any trouble," Kassidy said. "It'd be just like him to try to pull something like an apology on Christmas morning."

I took a deep breath. I was not going to freak out. He was Ryleigh's father, and if he was in town, I wouldn't deny him seeing her on Christmas. "I'm not falling for that again." Three years ago, when Ryleigh was a baby, I'd asked him for a trial separation. He'd shown up on Christmas with an epic apol-ogy, and for a few months, everything seemed great again. He was an attentive husband and doting father—until he met a flight attendant that caught his eye.

"Good," Khloe said. "'Cause I like Trask. And his family. Brooklyn and Brian are the sweetest couple, and their parents remind me so much of Mama and Daddy. They're a good family, Kami. It just thrills me that you managed to meet their son in some random restaurant clear across the country."

"A Godwink for sure," Mama said.

For sure, I thought. I texted Trask while they continued the conversation, wanting to push Sutton out of my mind. *What a priceless gift you've given me. I'm so glad to be home.* I wouldn't let Sutton get to me. I'd continue to take the high road.

It's my pleasure, he texted back right away.

I took a deep breath, and with the courage that comes from being on the other side of a screen texted, *I can't wait for tomorrow. It's been so long since I've danced. You dance, right?*

Even if I didn't, I'd try so I could hold you in my arms every chance I got.

I let out a long breath to steady my excitement. I hadn't even meant slow dancing, but now that's all I wanted to do.

"Look at you, Kami!" I jerked my head up from my phone toward Khloe. "You're blushing! Are you texting Trask?"

"Maybe." I looked back down at the phone to avoid the eyes staring at me.

Another text had come in. *Did I say something wrong?*

No, what you said was perfect. My family is with me ... They're teasing me because I'm grinning at my phone like a dummy.

Ah. I wish I could see that grin.

"Kamryn!"

I'll show it to you tomorrow. Gotta go!

"What?" I looked up, and they were all smiling at me.

It felt like a weight I didn't know I'd been holding had been lifted.

Later, visions of Trask filled my mind as I drifted off to sleep.

23

TRASK

*T*hree times, Brian's brother had to poke me to pay attention during the wedding ceremony. I stood in line with the groomsmen, angled toward the pastor, but my eyes and thoughts were focused elsewhere. It was difficult to concentrate on anything but Kami in the back row on the bride's side. She was about as far away from me as she could be, yet I saw her clearly.

I'd never seen her dressed up before, and if I wasn't half in love with her already, I was now. It seemed shallow to think that—being in love based on her beauty—but that's not how it was. But seeing her in an elegant gown with part of her hair piled on her head just made me crazier for her. I couldn't speak when I saw her, and there might have been drool involved because I was sure my mouth hung open for too long.

Instead of picking Kami up, I met her and Ryleigh at the bee farm, since it was just a short walk from her parents' house. She was going to go over early in case her sisters needed any last-minute help. Her willingness to help her family and make sacrifices for her daughter were qualities that made me even more willing to give this relationship a go.

It was a beautiful December day in the Lowcountry, just over sixty degrees with a light breeze. The daytime nuptials couldn't have been more picture-perfect. By the time we sat down for dinner, though, it was starting to cool off. When Kami rubbed her bare arms, I was quick to offer her my jacket. I'd just draped it over her shoulders when her sister—Kassidy, I think—came over to our table to whisper in her ear.

Her smile turned to a frown. "I'll be right back. Can you keep an eye on Ryleigh?"

I nodded, and Marsha gestured to the two little girls, who had commandeered the figurines from the cake topper and were acting out the wedding at their seats.

"I doubt she'll even realize you're gone," Chad joked.

"Thanks." They walked off hastily, and I turned my body to watch them disappear around the building toward the entrance.

"I wonder what that's about?" I asked. When she didn't return after five minutes, I started to get antsy. "Do you think I should check on her?"

"I hope it's not an emergency." My mother frowned. "Let me find out. I see Khloe just over there. Khloe, dear!"

Khloe looked up from a few tables away, where she was fixing a lopsided centerpiece of peonies, magnolias, and Spanish moss. Mama waved at her, and she hurried over.

"Your sisters disappeared a few minutes ago, and Trask is wondering if he should check on Kami?"

"Mama, I'm sure she's fine," I said. I didn't want Khloe to think I was troublesome.

"Actually—" Khloe looked right at me. "You might want to."

What wasn't she saying? I hoped everything was okay.

"I can do that. Out front?" I stood up.

She nodded. "I'll take you."

Khloe picked up her pace as we left the reception area. "Sutton is here," she said tightly.

My pulse quickened. We rounded the building, and the first thing I saw was Kami, shading her eyes with her hands. Her lips were set in a thin line as Sutton bent toward her, animated and angry.

He heard us approaching and pivoted on his heel. I squared my shoulders as he charged toward me. Khloe skirted around him and went directly to Kami.

"I want my daughter," he growled. "It's my right."

"Better check that paperwork again, Sutton," Kassidy called.

"I don't care about paperwork. You can't keep her from me. It's Christmas!"

"It's *not* Christmas, you big jerk." Khloe's heels clicked on the pavement as she came up behind him and poked him in the arm. "It's a wedding, and you're not invited. And unless you want to lose your invite to Christmas morning, you'd better leave before I call the cops."

"Graham's already on his way." Kassidy smirked and winked at me behind Sutton's back. "Dating a deputy has its perks."

"You ready to go back in, Kami?" I asked over her shoulder, completely ignoring him.

"She's not yours." He lifted a fist.

"You don't want to do that, man," I said.

"I could kill you with my bare hands right now if I wanted to," Sutton growled.

I held his gaze, challenging him to try. His eyes were wild with rage. He might have learned some lethal maneuvers in the military, but by the time I finished college, I'd earned a third-degree black belt and was sure I could hold my own against him.

"Don't you dare threaten him!" Kami sprang from Kassidy's arms and was in between us before I could blink. "Sutton Spencer, you leave here *now*. Stop trying to make me feel guilty. I don't owe you anything. You cheated on me, remember? I do not belong to you, and if you don't watch it, I'll get a restraining order and a lawyer and God help you if you ever want to see Ryleigh again!"

The flashing lights of a police cruiser turning in to the back of the parking lot punctuated her warning.

"Oh good, here's my man now." Kassidy waved to the car.

"This isn't over, Kamryn," Sutton spat, taking a step back.

"It had better be." I reached around Kami's waist and pulled her to my side.

"Are you threatening me, hockey boy? I'll snap your wrist so fast—"

"That's enough!" Kami began to shake. "We don't have to stand here and listen to this. C'mon, Trask. Graham will deal with him."

She took my hand and gripped it tightly. At the entrance to the main building, she punched in a code by the door and drew me inside. I took in the shelves of honey, tables of candles, soap, and other products, and a long wooden counter with a cash register and clear jars filled with multicolored honey sticks.

She spoke breathlessly. "I just need a minute before we go back out there. I can meet you if you want to go ahead without—"

"Whoa, hey." I squeezed her hand, then let it go to cup her cheeks. I wanted her to look into my eyes and know that I was in this no matter what her ex tried to pull. He wouldn't scare me off. "Look at me, Kam."

Her lashes lifted, revealing the water pooling in her eyes. I drew her head to my lips and gently kissed her forehead. A tear dripped onto my chin.

"I'm sorry," she breathed. "I never thought he would show up here—"

"It's okay. It's going to be okay." I pulled her into my arms. It was quiet enough to hear the faint sounds of Phil Collins's "You'll Be in My Heart." I smiled. "Do you hear that?" I whispered.

She looked up. "The *Tarzan* song?"

"Yeah. They're doing the father-daughter dance."

"To the *Tarzan* song?"

"Have I mentioned my family is Disney-obsessed?"

She chuckled. "No wonder you didn't balk at dressing like Captain Hook. You probably already owned that costume, didn't you?" she teased.

"I plead the fifth."

"If they play 'Second Star to the Right,' Ryleigh's gonna go nuts."

"I'm sure we can arrange it."

"Awesome." She squeezed her arms around my middle, and it made me feel all warm inside. "Thanks for being here, Trask."

I smiled. "Shouldn't I be saying that to you?"

She laughed. "You know what I mean. C'mon. Let's not miss this. I bet there's not a dry eye in the garden."

"I bet you're right."

Hand in hand, we walked back to the reception. The sun was beginning to set, and the twinkle lights lit up the palms and greenery, setting a scene right out of a fairy tale.

"Your sisters knocked it out of the park," I whispered. Ryleigh sat with Mylee at the edge of the floor, and we stood behind Marsha and Chad as the song wrapped up. Kami was right—everyone gathered around the dance floor was either crying or looked like they were about to.

The song transitioned into Rascal Flatts's "My Wish," and Brian led his mother around the floor. Kami leaned into my side, and I put my arm around her. I wondered if she was thinking about her wedding to Sutton and what she'd looked like dressed up in white. Watching Brooklyn and Brian today, it wouldn't even cross my mind that in just a few years they could be divorced and battling for custody over kids they didn't even have yet.

The song began to fade out, and Brian's mother waved to Brooklyn to join them for the last few notes. Applause rippled, and the DJ came on the mic to make a few announcements.

"We're gonna get this party started with some favorites to get you moving! Do not go back to your seats—I repeat, do not go back to your seats! And pay attention—we're mixing it up with some cool tunes!"

"Let me see your dance moves," Kami said, tugging me onto the floor for an all-too-familiar line dance tune.

"How 'bout I get you a drink?" I teased, purposely wanting her to react.

"Trask!" She laughed, poking my bicep and challenging me with her expression.

I laughed. "Kidding!" I unbuttoned my sleeves and rolled them up my arms. "Let's do this!"

I think she was surprised by how well I could keep up, and when the DJ finally slowed it down with a country ballad, I nearly whooped for joy. Not because the dancing had been a workout—I'd barely broken a sweat—but because I wanted to hold her so badly.

"Every time I hear this song, I'm going to think of you, and us, right here." I hugged her close as we swayed to the music.

"Butterflies." She leaned into me. I loved how we fit together. "One of my favorite songs."

I let go of her waist and tucked a lock of hair behind her ear so I could see her face. "And now it's one of mine."

KAMI

*T*he skin around my ear tingled with Trask's touch. I was having trouble breathing under the weight of his stare. It was so intense, I couldn't speak, either.

"Kami?" Trask whispered, lowering his head.

"Yeah?"

"Can I ... Can I kiss you? Here?"

"On the dance floor?"

His eyes shone with such sincerity, it only took me a second to decide. This was the moment I wanted to get caught up in. The way he looked at me ... Sutton had never looked at me like *that*. Holy Jesus. Secret-ish dating be damned. I was going to let Trask kiss me and didn't care who knew about it.

He stared at me like I mattered, like I was the *only* thing that mattered. I'd only seen this look once before, which is how I knew what it was.

It was the way my parents looked at each other. Still, after almost thirty years of marriage, my daddy looked at my mama the way Trask was looking at me now.

I nodded my consent and swallowed as I tilted my chin up.

I felt safe in his arms. His lips crashed down on mine. Warm and soft, he pressed gently and tightened his arms around my waist. The weight of his body against mine caused a surge of desire I wasn't prepared for and inspired me to deepen the kiss.

He responded, and we dueled for control of the kiss. This was far more intense than our make-out session by the Christmas tree. More intentional. I felt like we were setting a new standard in kissing. I'd never been kissed so deliberately, with such tenderness. I was awed, overwhelmed, and unaware that we were making a spectacle.

"Mr. Tiggerman! Why are you kissing my Mommy?"

I snickered into the kiss and ended it with a final smooch so he could answer to Ryleigh. She looked up at him, hands on her hips. Mylee was next to her, biting her bottom lip and glaring at him through slitted eyes.

He shrugged. "I thought she needed to be kissed."

"Why?"

"Because ..."

"Yeah, Trask, why?" Marsha grinned from behind her brother.

"Don't you start, Marsh. Because ... Because I like your mom a lot, Ryleigh."

"Hmm." She turned to Mylee. "I don't know about this."

Trask's lips twitched. "Well, I do, and I think it's great. And I think you're pretty great, too." She beamed back at me, and her approval meant everything.

Mylee began jumping and pulled on Trask's sleeve. "Uncle Trask! Listen! It's our song! You can't dance with Ryleigh's mommy to *our song!*"

"That would not be a good idea." I winked at him, familiar with New Kids on the Block's "My Favorite Girl."

"Pick me up, Uncle Trask!"

I took Ryleigh back to the table as Trask danced with his niece, singing the words to her. He was full of surprises.

"Mommy, your purse is wiggly," Ryleigh said.

I opened it to find my phone buzzing with a call from Bonnie Spencer. I swiped to turn it off. I checked my messages. Three missed texts from Sutton and two from his mother.

No, thanks. I'd read them tomorrow. Maybe. I let Sutton ruin enough of my day already.

I put my phone back into my purse and pulled Ryleigh onto my lap to watch Trask and Mylee, who were now the only people on the dance floor.

"I fixed it. Are you getting tired, Ryleigh?"

"No." After she said it, she yawned.

I hugged her close, and we just sat there, content, until Trask, Mylee, Marsha, and Chad returned to the table.

"Ryleigh! They're going to cut the cake!" Mylee said. "Auntie Brooklyn said we can help!"

Ryleigh jumped from my lap. I smiled shyly at Trask, and he lowered himself into the seat next to me. "New Kids, huh?"

"My mama's a Blockhead." He shrugged.

I giggled. We watched the cake-cutting, and I ignored the buzzing coming from my purse. When I saw Kassidy heading toward our table with a troubled expression, I was suddenly filled with a sense of dread. Her face was tight, and I knew it was somehow related to the calls I wasn't answering.

She sat down next to me in Ryleigh's vacant chair. I felt

Trask lean in behind me, and his hand found mine. He must have felt it too.

"What is it?" I whispered, bracing myself.

"Um, I just spoke with Graham. The fire department just pulled Sutton's old truck out of Shaftesbury Pond. He was racing Scooter Hodges, and he went off the bridge ..."

I stared at her and gripped Trask's hand as tight as I could. My marriage and love for Sutton ended long ago, but he gave me Ryleigh. He was still her father, and I didn't want anything bad to happen to him. "Is he ...is he ...?"

She shook her head. "He's alive, but he swallowed a lot of water before Scooter could get to him and pull him out. A few broken ribs. He's at the hospital ... in a coma."

My free hand flew to my mouth as my stomach roiled. I couldn't believe this was happening. What happened if he died?

And what was I going to tell Ryleigh?

25

TRASK

"*T*ell me how I can help. Can I bring you to the hospital?"

Kami shuddered and didn't answer.

I looked up at Kassidy. "What can I do?"

"Do you want us to bring Ryleigh home?" Marsha asked. "Or she can stay with us if your parents want to, um, go to the hospital."

Kami shook her head, and I loosened my grip as she stood up. "No. I'll call Mama and Daddy to come get her. Kass, do they know?"

"I'm sure Bonnie has called them by now. You might want to check your phone."

"Yes. Yes, I need to check my messages." She stared at her purse, then turned around to hug me. "I'm so sorry to put a black cloud over your sister's wedding. Please, don't leave. I'll get a ride over there." She took her purse from the table and turned back to Kassidy. "Do you think Graham can bring me?"

"*I* can bring you, Kami." I wanted to be with her and was sure Brooklyn wouldn't mind if I left.

"No." Her bottom lip trembled. "I'll feel bad forever if you leave before this is over. I'll call you later, okay?" Her voice cracked.

I pulled her in for a hug and whispered directly into her ear. "You call me for anything, anytime. If I don't hear from you by the time the wedding is over, I'm going to the hospital so I can be there for you."

"Okay."

I let her go and kissed her gently on her lips. Then I wrapped my arms around her to remind her she wasn't alone. I just wanted to hold her for a moment.

"Bye, Trask." She wiped her eyes and followed Kassidy out.

I wished I was bringing her. I wanted to comfort her and tell her everything would be okay. And a part of me needed to know what she was thinking and if she still had feelings for the guy. Her gut reaction made me uneasy. She'd been shocked, and it looked like she was struggling to hold herself together. I knew they'd known each other for a long time, and while I didn't think most people wished their exes were dead, especially not if they had kids, maybe underneath it all, she still cared for him and wished things hadn't had to end.

Before my thoughts could spiral into a black hole of the worst things, I decided to go find my dad. He could always help me make sense of things when I didn't have a clear head.

I found him smoking a cigar with Brian on the far side of the garden. "Hey, Dad. Hey, Bri. Congrats again, man. Welcome to the family." He offered me a cigar, but I shook my head.

I didn't want to dampen Brian's big day, so after a few minutes of small talk, I went to find Mylee. There were only about another forty minutes until the reception ended. She could keep me distracted till then.

I found her and Ryleigh on a stone bench with Marsha. They were twisting flowers into some kind of rope.

"Look, Mr. Tiggerman! Mylee's mommy showed us how to make a daisy chain! But there's not any daisies here so we have honeywort! Isn't that a funny name for a flower? Warts are so gross, but these flowers are pretty."

"It's very funny. Can I help?" I wanted to protect her, and if what I had to do right now involved weaving flowers, I would weave flowers.

Mylee regarded me carefully. "Only if you promise to try your very best. All the boys I know like to squish flowers!"

"Mylee," Marsha chided. "Not *all* the boys you know. Your daddy doesn't squish flowers."

She shrugged. "That's 'cause he's a man."

Marsha snorted. I didn't know whether or not to feel insulted.

Not long after, the DJ called for the last dance. I checked my watch. Almost eight. At least it was still early. A moth fluttered by, and I remembered it was less than an hour ago Kami and I were having the perfect night. We even had a song.

I hadn't heard from her, so I called after we gathered around Brooklyn and Brian to send them off. It went to voicemail, so I sent a text.

Are you okay? I'm on my way.

I waited for a response, and when it didn't come, I said goodbye to everyone and headed for the parking lot. I'd rented an SUV with a car seat, and it felt incredibly empty being in it alone.

THE WOMAN AT THE INFORMATION DESK GAVE ME A ONCE-OVER. I was still in my tux, minus the jacket.

"Let me guess," she said. "You're here to see Sutton Spencer."

"How'd you know?" I asked.

"I went to school with him and Kami. She's up there with his parents. Said a tall guy named Trask might be along. You look like a Trask. Got an ID?"

I took out my wallet and showed it to her. "Can you tell me where to find her?"

"ICU waiting room. That's as far as you can go."

"Thanks."

I took the elevator up and followed the signs. Kami was sitting in a recliner in the back corner. Her eyes were closed as she leaned against the wall next to her chair. I sat down next to her, not wanting to wake her up.

"I'm not sleeping. I'm just resting my eyes," she mumbled. I took a closer look. She looked exhausted. My heart ached for her.

"It's okay. I can just sit here with you while you rest."

"Trask?" She opened her eyes but didn't move.

"Yeah?" I wanted to pull her to me or at least hold her hand and tell her everything was going to be all right.

"I meant to text you. I guess I fell asleep."

"It's okay. I'm here now." And I'd stay for as long as she wanted me to.

"But you don't need to be. This isn't your problem. And it's Christmas Eve. I'm sure you want to spend time with your family."

"Kami, I—" How could I explain to her that she was all that mattered to me right now?

"You should go." She sat up straight and gripped the wooden arms of the chair.

I stiffened. "Why? Do you want to be alone?"

She pressed her lips together and her fingertips to her temples. "I think I need to be. It's just—this is all … this is all too much for me right now. He still has me as his medical power of attorney. There's so much paperwork. I can't think."

"You don't have to think." I reached for her hand, but she stood up and began pacing.

"Yes, I do! What if he dies? Then what? What happens to me and Ryleigh? What if I have to make a decision that ends his life? I can't even imagine how she'll feel and how messed up she'll be if her dad dies, and I'm the one who has to decide it!" She stopped mid-stride and covered her face with her hands, choking back sobs. "Can you imagine if your daddy died and it was your mama who pulled the plug? My whole world would have been crushed if I lost my daddy at her age, and if I knew my mama—I don't know what to do if I have to make that decision—and if he—if he dies—and money is already tight—I feel awful thinking this, but what if I have to leave my doctorate program? How will I support Ryleigh?" She glared at the floor. "That stupid, stupid, selfish man!"

I flew to my feet and took her in my arms. "I want to help. Let me help, Kami."

She pushed at my chest and stepped back. "No. Thank you, but—no. You can't help us. There isn't anything for you to do.

I …" We jumped at the voices outside the door, and she sprang away from me as an older couple entered the room. "Please, Trask." She lowered her voice. "Go home to your family and let me deal with mine. I'll call you when I get it all sorted."

I read between the lines, and the finality of her instruction crushed me like the weight of a pile of opposing players.

26

KAMI

I watched Trask walk down the hall, shoulders slumped and hands in his pockets. It felt awful sending him away, but I just didn't know what to do with him. I certainly couldn't lean on him with Sutton's parents in the room. I didn't want to cause them any further distress. His mother still held out hope for us. There wasn't any, but it felt like I'd be rubbing salt in her wound if I leaned on Trask, especially if I had to—

No. I wasn't going to think about Sutton not making it.

I could be strong by myself. And I had Ryleigh to think about, first and foremost.

But I couldn't imagine what his parents were going through. The possibility of losing a child—their only child—I couldn't even. If it had been Ryleigh … Oh my God, if Ryleigh had been with him! I almost retched at the thought.

What had he been thinking? He'd been mad, sure, but he hadn't been reckless since high school, and even then nothing truly serious that could land him in jail or risk his future military career. I'd thought the Air Force had put an end to his posturing and devil-may-care attitude. Unless it'd just been camouflaged this whole time.

I had loved him once, and thought he was a good man. He loved Ryleigh, even though he often seemed to get his priorities out of order. I didn't want anything bad to happen to him.

I thought I'd worked past my pain and disappointment. Now, with him possibly dying, I realized I still had a long way to go to make sense of how the boy I fell so desperately in love with could grow into a man who made me feel like garbage. Seeing him lying helpless in the ICU, all banged up ... he looked so young. I wondered when his mental state had shifted and why.

My wounded heart ached for our daughter and the thought of her growing up without her dad. I knew for a fact I was over him, and I'd long since mourned the plans we'd made to build a life together. Was it okay to be upset over someone who had shown me time and time again how little I mattered to him?

Unlike Trask, who showed me I mattered to him every day. Sutton had had his chance, and it was time for me to go for my second one.

"Kamryn." Sutton's mother pulled me out of my thoughts. I was still standing by the door, staring out the window to the now-empty hallway.

I felt a hand on my shoulder. "It's for the best, dear. I'm sure that boy doesn't want it on his conscience to break up a family that should be together."

Spinning around, I glared at her, surprised by the unexpected vitriol coursing through me. "He wouldn't. It was *your son* that broke up this family. Trask is my friend, and if I decide I want him to become more than that, it's none of your damn business."

She blinked at me. I'd never spoken to her that way in all the years I'd known her.

I wouldn't apologize.

I considered giving up my turn to sit with Sutton, but I didn't think he should be alone. A nurse waved me through, and I went straight to the chair by his bed. This big protector that used to hold all my hopes and dreams was wrapped in bandages from head to toe and connected to more machines than I could count. And if he woke up alone and then died, I'd regret not having this time. I wanted him to wake up for Ryleigh and to solidify the closure between us.

"Kami, dear. Wake up, honey."

"Mama? What are you doing here?" I rubbed my eyes. Sutton's room was dark. "What time is it?"

"It's just after one in the morning. I brought you a change of clothes, but I was hoping you'd come home with me."

"I don't know … should I?"

She sat down next to me and looked Sutton over. "You absolutely should. There isn't anything for you to do here. Don't put him before Ryleigh. And you've got a full day planned with your family. And when he wakes up, you make that man sign the papers that transfer the decisions about his care to his mama. I've got my whole prayer group praying that he wakes up and has his come-to-Jesus moment. Sometimes you have to hit rock bottom to realize the treasures you neglected along the way."

"Mama, even if he does, I'm not getting back with him."

"That's not where I was going with that, sweetheart. He needs to shape up to be the best daddy for Ryleigh. His chapter with you is over. You know that, and I'm certain of it, too. But he's got a whole book to write with his little girl. And it needs to be a happy one."

"I really hope so, Mama." I stood up and stretched. "If you think it's okay for me to go home—"

"I do. His parents aren't going to leave him right now, and Bonnie told me extended family and friends have set up a schedule to sit with him all day tomorrow. Can you believe they called your sisters?" She chuckled. "I think you can imagine Kassidy's reply."

I laughed. "She never did care much for him."

"No, she never has. But I caught her praying for him." She winked.

It dawned on me then that Sutton might be able to hear us talking. I leaned over to take his left hand in both of mine. "Sutton, I—" I swallowed. "You need to get through this. Please. Ryleigh loves you so much. She needs her daddy." I gasped when his fingers twitched in my hand. "Sutton? Can you hear me? Are you awake?"

No response. I sighed. "I guess I'm ready to go. Can you bring me back tomorrow before company comes?"

"Of course."

On the way back to my parents' house, I checked my messages. So many texts. Only one from Trask, a string of praying hands and heart emojis. A couple each from Kassidy, Khloe, and Brenna, who Trask had been keeping updated, and several from local friends and family. I read through them all but didn't respond to any. I was so mentally drained, I could barely form a sentence. I'd write back tomorrow.

By the time I crawled into my old bed next to a sprawled-out Ryleigh, it was nearly 2 a.m. She'd be awake in just a few hours, and I had no idea what I was going to tell her.

My ringing phone woke me up, and I reached to grab it before it disturbed Ryleigh. My heart thundered as I swiped, dreading the possibility of the worst news.

Instead of the hospital or Bonnie, it was Khloe. I sat up and noted the absence of Ryleigh. Sunshine streamed through the slats in the partially opened blinds.

"Thought you might want to get out of bed before lunch."

I yawned. "What time is it? Where's Ryleigh?"

"Almost eleven, and she's baking cookies with Mama and Grandpa Silly."

"Oh shoot!" I tossed the covers to the side and ran to my suitcase, pulling out clothes. "I wanted to go to the hospital before Grandpa Silly and the rest of the family gets here!"

"You needed your sleep. Even Ryleigh thought so. She woke me up before seven and told me you were snoring and wouldn't stop."

I cringed. "Sorry?"

She laughed. "No worries! You know I'll miss her when y'all go back to Colorado."

"I know. But we'll be home for good soon."

"Hmm. I'm not so sure of that."

I dropped the clothes I'd chosen on the bed. "No? Why not?"

"Trask. You've got it bad for him, Kam. And it's mutual. Don't let that fish go."

"But—"

"No buts. Speaking of, he's called me twice this morning.

Wants to know if he can come by. I told him I'd have you call him when you woke up."

"Thanks. Let me get dressed. I'll be down in a few minutes."

I ended the call, threw my clothes on and ran into the bathroom to make myself presentable. I texted Bonnie on my way downstairs and asked for updates. Nothing new.

My parents convinced me to stay home and visit with the family. There really wasn't anything I could do at the hospital, and besides, what would I tell Ryleigh if I left? Everyone had been instructed not to mention anything to her. She was too little to understand, and she wasn't allowed in the ICU. I wouldn't want her to see her dad like that anyway. The way he looked ... it would haunt me forever, and I was a grown adult. Ryleigh didn't need that image burned in her brain.

I texted Trask, and he asked if he could come by today. I wasn't ready for him to meet Sutton's parents, so tomorrow morning wouldn't work. I decided tonight was better and would cause me less stress until I figured out what to do about Sutton.

I went into the kitchen to join in on the cookie-baking chaos. My grandfather was there, and Ryleigh had put him in charge of drawing smiley faces on the gingerbread men before she doused them in too many sprinkles.

Trask arrived and fit right in, chatting with my grandparents and even helping Ryleigh mix together reindeer food. She'd made some at school but left it in Sutton's car. Ryleigh told Trask about the oat and glitter mix, worried about Santa's beloved animals flying on an empty stomach. He suggested carrots as a healthier alternative and complained good-naturedly when she insisted on adding the "pixie dust." I giggled when I saw some in his hair, and I took pleasure in combing it out with my fingers.

The afternoon passed too quickly, and there were moments I completely forgot about Sutton and enjoyed myself. Then I'd find myself comparing the two and then felt guilty because Sutton could be dying.

After an enjoyable dinner set to a playlist of Ryleigh's favorite Disney Princess Christmas songs, we all settled in the family room. Khloe appeared in the doorway and held up a book. "I thought since all of us are here, we could pick up on an old family tradition. Who wants to read first?"

"Me! I know this book!" Ryleigh abandoned the tiny dolls and princess houses under the tree that were currently serving as a Christmas village and ran to Khloe. "Can I please read, Auntie Khloe?"

"Of course, but you have to sit. And after you read the first page, you pass the book so we all get a chance to read."

"Okay!" She ran to the couch, where Trask and I were sitting, and climbed up between us. "Now?" Khloe brought her the book, and she accepted it gleefully.

"I didn't know you could read," Trask said, leaning over her.

"I read pictures," she said offhandedly as she thumbed through the first few pages.

"Ah," he said. I caught his gaze and smiled. He winked back, and I felt a little bit of the stress leaving my body.

"I'm ready! Is everybody listening? Grandma and Grandpa, eyes on me! Mimi and PopPop, please stop talking. Aunties, please put your screens down. And Grandpa Silly, WAKE UP!"

Kassidy poked our grandfather gently. He startled awake, and we all laughed.

"Go ahead, Ryleigh," I encouraged.

She cleared her throat dramatically. "It was the night before Christmas, and aaaaaaaaaall through the house, everyone was sleeping." She pointed to the picture. "The mommy and the daddy were sleeping. And the kids were sleeping. The cat was sleeping. Even the mouse was sleeping!" She passed the book to Trask. "Your turn. Mommy can go last. She's done this before." I stifled a giggle as Trask accepted the book.

His rich baritone filled the room. I closed my eyes. I could listen to him read forever. "The stockings were hung by the chimney with care, in hopes that St. Nicholas soon would be there."

"Santa has *so* many names! Mr. Tiggerman, now you pass the book to Auntie Kassidy."

He obliged, and the book made its way around. Ryleigh fell asleep toward the end, and Trask carried her to bed.

Her little voice was barely audible as she mumbled into his sleeve. "One more sleep 'til Christmas, Tig-man," she whispered.

"That's right, baby," he whispered, pressing his eyes closed.

The way he cradled her in his arms, then gently laid her down touched me so deeply I couldn't speak as a realization crashed into me full-speed.

He loved my little girl.

Trask's strong arm snaked around my waist and pulled me to him. I leaned my head on his shoulder, and we watched Ryleigh sleep for a few minutes.

"I guess I should go."

"Mmm." I mumbled into his shoulder. Despite the fun day together, there was still a cloud hanging over us. I was still in a bit of a somber mood and hated feeling so un-Christmassy. Ryleigh didn't know her dad was hurt, and I dreaded telling her.

"Or," he whispered into my hair. The vibrations of his voice incited goosebumps down my neck and arms.

"Or?" I whispered, looking up at him. His eyes sparkled, reflecting in the soft glow of the nearby nightlight.

"I could help get ready for Santa."

I smiled. "Follow me."

Slipping my hand in his, I led him back down the stairs where my family was cleaning up from the day's festivities. After we said goodbye to my grandparents, I led Trask into the garage and pointed to my old hope chest. Purged of memories from my first marriage, it now held Ryleigh's Christmas gifts.

He let go of my hand and lifted the lid to reveal brightly wrapped princess-themed Christmas paper. "Nice. Reminds me…I have a little gift I got for Ryleigh. It didn't arrive until after I left to come over here. Is it okay if I bring it by tomorrow?"

"That was sweet of you," I said. Sutton's parents still planned to come over early to watch Ryleigh open her Santa gifts. "I'm not sure what our plans for the day are yet. Can I call you after Ryleigh opens her presents?"

"Sure," he said, but he looked away. I could tell by his tone he was disappointed. I loved how much he cared for my girl and me, but we were in rough waters right now, and I didn't know how to navigate them.

While we arranged the gifts, one by one, my family popped

in to say goodnight. When everything was set, I walked Trask out, and we shared a long goodnight kiss on the front porch. On the lawn, Ryleigh's reindeer food glittered in the moonlight.

He pulled away, and I wrapped my arms around him. "I know things are still kind of up in the air with you going back to Colorado," he said. "Would you like me to rebook your flight on the twenty-sixth to a later date?"

I leaned into him as it hit me. I didn't know how long I'd need to stay here. If Sutton didn't make it ... I shuddered. I'd have to call Brenna to find coverage for me at Brewski's. "Yes, please."

"Okay, any idea for when?"

I shook my head. "Maybe you should just cancel it? I'll book my own flight when I know." I cringed, thinking about what the cost would do to my already-hurting bank account.

"Okay. Um... Do you think you'll be back for New Year's? Coach is having a party."

"I hope so, but...I don't know. Things are so uncertain right now."

"I understand. I hate this for you, Kami. You and Ryleigh should be having the best Christmas, and instead...I'm sorry."

"Thanks for being here, Trask." I looked up into his beautiful face. I wanted so much more with him. I knew he understood Ryleigh was my number one priority, and part of that was making sure she had a relationship with her father. I wished, not for the first time, that things weren't so complicated.

He held my gaze, and my heart thumped, waiting for him to reply. Instead, he nodded, kissed me on the cheek, and let go. My eyes watered as I watched him jog down the porch steps and to his old pickup. He waved before he got in, and I lifted my hand as he drove off.

I pulled my sweater tightly around me, immediately aware of the loss of Trask's warmth.

27

TRASK

I couldn't remember a Christmas morning that had ever felt this un-Christmassy. I went through the motions on autopilot, never feeling authentically present. My mind wasn't there, and I couldn't put my heart into celebrating knowing that Kami was suffering and my sweet little Ryleigh-girl might lose her dad.

The whole family came over for a late breakfast. Mylee brought a huge bag of new toys and from Santa, and I distracted myself helping Chad put them together. When I hadn't heard an update by early afternoon, I drove out to Kami's parents' place. She'd mentioned Sutton's parents would be there in the morning, so I hoped they'd be gone by the time I arrived. I hated to see her so down, and I wanted to be there to support her.

As I pulled up in front of the house, an older couple I assumed were his parents were loading their car. I waited on the street for them to vacate the driveway. The woman saw me and walked over to my driver's-side window. I lowered it and waited.

She'd been crying, but she was smiling. "I imagine you've heard about our Christmas miracle! Sutton has woken up!"

"That's wonderful news, ma'am." I hadn't heard. Kami hadn't returned any of my calls or texts since yesterday. I still cared about her and Ryleigh. She had to know that. And I hoped she still cared about me.

"It's the best news. Praise the Lord!" She leaned in, forcing me to look directly at her.

My nerves tingled, already on edge and in defense mode. "It sure is." I glanced toward the house.

"Listen, Trask, right? I'm sure you're a nice man. Kamryn wouldn't befriend someone who wasn't. But you must know that's all you can have with her. A friendship. She and my Sutton were meant to be together. You shouldn't try to break up this family."

"Listen, ma'am, with all due respect—"

"No, you listen. You have a big career ahead of you. Go back to Colorado and let this family heal."

I just stared at her. I was so angry, I couldn't form words.

"Is that a gift for Ryleigh? I can take it in for you."

Next to me on the seat was a robotic puppy gift-wrapped in fairy paper. How astute.

"I can give it to her myself."

"I'm afraid you can't. They've already left for the hospital."

I was done with this woman. "Then I'll go there. Merry Christmas."

I rolled up my window before she could reply, put the car in reverse, and sped around her without looking back.

I texted Kami from the parking lot. *I'm at the hospital.*

The same woman was at the information desk. "He's been moved to a regular room. You can go on up. Room 347."

I peeked into the room. Ryleigh was in bed with Sutton in her Christmas dress, headphones on, sucking her thumb and watching something on the television. Kami and Sutton were talking. I was about to knock on the door when Sutton's voice got louder. I froze.

"Please, Kam? I need you."

"You don't need me. You've never needed me."

It was like watching a train wreck. He turned toward her and grabbed her hand in desperation. "Please, I want us to be a family again. I know I've messed up so many times. I'll earn your forgiveness and your trust again, I promise."

"Sutton—"

"Kami, I love you!"

I couldn't hear anymore. Maybe I didn't want to wait for her reply. I knocked on the door.

Loudly. Even Ryleigh heard it. Three heads turned my way.

"Mr. Tiggerman!" Ryleigh scrambled off the bed and ran toward me.

I put her gift on the counter by the door and crouched to catch her in my arms. "Merry Christmas, sweet girl." I pulled her close and closed my eyes. I had the worst feeling this hug would have to last a long time. I couldn't get choked up, at least not here.

She wiggled out of my grasp and pointed to the gift. "Is that for me?"

"It is. Ask your Mommy if you can open it." I stood up tall and took in the scene before me. Sutton was definitely banged up. And definitely alive. He glared at me like any strong, healthy male would glare at his competition.

"Trask." Kami stood up and walked over to me. Her eyes

brightened and locked on mine. "Thanks for coming. I was going to call you when I left here."

"Mommy!"

"You can open it, Ryleigh."

"It's okay. I know it's a bad time. I just wanted to bring Ryleigh her gift. Do you want me to come by your parents' house later? When it's a better time?"

She sighed and shook her head. "No. I'm not sure what we're doing later. So much is still up in the air."

"I'm sure. But now that he's awake ... Will you be coming home with me tomorrow?"

"No. I can't go back to Colorado yet. They'll release him tomorrow, but he'll have to stay in South Carolina for a while. Ryleigh needs to spend time with him. This coming weekend is his weekend with her and—" She looked back at him.

"Mommy! Daddy! It's a puppy! Oh, *thank you*, Mr. Tiggerman!" Ryleigh flew to my arms. "Santa didn't bring me one. Grandpa Silly said he probably just forgotted and maybe he'll 'member next year. But I like this one!"

"Yeah? I'm glad. What are you going to name it?"

She cocked her head in thought, then jumped in excitement. "Tigger Bale!"

Kami's snort set off the three of us into laughter.

"Sure, just act like I'm not even here." Sutton pouted. "Steal my family from right under my nose."

Both Ryleigh and Kami stiffened. I spoke softly to Kami. "I can get some time off to stay here with you. I want to support you."

"No, Trask. Your team needs you."

What she didn't say was clear: She didn't need me. I felt them slipping away from me, and it ripped my heart in two.

"Message heard," I said tightly. "I'll see you when I see you." I bent down to Ryleigh, who was clutching her puppy with one arm and her mother's leg with the other. "Merry Christmas, Ryleigh." I kissed her head, stood up, and strode out the door without looking back.

Third "no" in a row. It was barely a breakup because we hadn't really had a chance to get started.

So why did this breakup hurt worse than the last two?

28

KAMI

I felt awful sending Trask away. I was really messing things up. Everything seemed to be on fire around me. I was used to being in control, and I needed to find a way to regain it. I couldn't ask Trask to stay with me, not at the risk of his career. It was midway through hockey season, and every game counted leading up to the playoffs.

Right after he left, my in-laws showed up. I needed to get out of there. "Ryleigh, baby, say goodbye to your daddy and then Grandma and Grandpa will take you into the hall to wait for Mommy, okay?"

Bonnie opened her mouth to protest, but I stared her down. I lifted Ryleigh to kiss her father on the cheek so that she wouldn't hurt his ribs and then waited until the door closed behind her to say my peace.

"I'm leaving. We'll stay for a few days, but then we're going back. If you have to stay here longer to heal, we'll figure something out."

"How can you be so cold, Kam? I almost died."

"Because of your own stupidity! What you should be asking me is how can I ever trust you with Ryleigh again!"

He had the decency to wince. "I'm sorry. That was a stupid thing to do. But it changed me, Kamryn. I'm serious. Can't we just forget the past? I promise I—"

"No. I've heard this all before, Sutton. So many times." I was so tired of his broken promises. He looked and sounded sincere, but it was too late for us. "You need to sign those papers." I glanced at them on the counter, untouched.

"But this time I mean it. Love can make this work."

"But I don't love you, Sutton." It felt freeing to say it out loud. I cared for him, but I didn't love him. Not at all.

And I have big feelings for Trask.

And I'd sent him away.

I thought it was for the best. My life was a mess, and he didn't deserve another man's leftovers. Sutton had broken me, and I was still struggling to put myself back together. Trask deserved someone who was whole, who hadn't made the mistakes I'd made or already failed at love and marriage.

But I wanted to be with Trask. I loved him. I was certain of it.

When Ryleigh and I arrived back at my parents' house, I noticed a small bubble envelope in the mail bowl with my name on it. Odd. I didn't remember shipping anything that small here. All of Ryleigh's and my family's gifts had arrived and been wrapped and unwrapped. I stuffed it into my sweater pocket to open later.

Ryleigh and I spent the rest of the day with my sisters and parents, stuffing our faces with sweets, playing my ancient version of Candyland, and watching Christmas movies. Kassidy left to go to Graham's family, and after dinner, we walked the neighborhood to look at the Christmas lights. Ryleigh skipped ahead with Mama and Daddy, and Khloe and I followed.

"Did you get your package?" she asked.

"I did. I can't believe they delivered on Christmas."

"I had to sign for it. What was so important you needed it today?"

I blinked at her. "I have no idea."

"You forgot what you ordered?"

"I guess so." I took the small bubble envelope out of my pocket and turned it over in my hand. "I really don't know what it could be."

"Well, open it, then."

I slid my finger under the transparent tab and pulled the strip across the top of the envelope. Inside was a small velvet drawstring bag and a slip of paper. I turned the paper over and read the note.

Kami,

I think of our song every time I see a butterfly, and I hope to hold you in my arms again soon.

Love, Trask

I stopped short on the sidewalk and passed the note and envelope to Khloe. My hand shook as I opened the small pouch and dumped the contents into my left hand. It was a bracelet. A delicate silver butterfly charm held together two chains of silver and sparkled with clear gemstones.

It was gorgeous.

And I was a fool.

THE NEXT DAY, AFTER ANOTHER FRUSTRATING VISIT WITH Sutton that served to confirm I was an even bigger fool letting Trask go, I dropped Ryleigh off with my parents and drove into Charleston. I needed to clear my head, and the route along the waterfront always helped.

Brilliant sunlight sparkled on the water to my right, and to my left, the park and homes on the South Battery looked picture-perfect decorated for Christmas.

"Charleston. That's where I'm from. Right on the South Battery."

I suddenly needed to see Trask. Frantically, I searched for a parking spot. His flight didn't leave for a few hours yet. I found a spot and pulled up the search engine on my phone to find his address. It was only a couple of blocks away.

I pulled out of the spot and let the GPS guide me to a familiar Colonial Revival just a short stroll from my favorite gardens. How many times had I walked past this house with friends and family over the years?

I pulled into the drive behind his pickup and got out. The house was gorgeous, in need of new paint, but the structure was in good condition. As I climbed the steps, the front door opened.

"Mrs. Emerson!" I grinned. "Hi!"

"Kami, dear, how lovely to see you." She smiled back, but stood stiffly. Without makeup on, she looked older and more frail. "You've just missed him. The ride-share picked him up about twenty minutes ago."

"Oh." I was too late. "Right." I smiled again, but was sure she caught the disappointment in my face. "I meant to call him earlier, but—"

She held up her hand. "You don't have to explain. He knows you have a lot on your mind."

"I do. And he's a big part of it." *Getting bigger and bigger each day.* "I need him to know that."

"I'm sure he knows it. Would you like to come in for tea or coffee?"

"I'd love to."

29

TRASK

I loosened my tie as I stepped into the plane at the Colorado Springs airport. Our chartered flight was headed to Missoula, Montana, where we'd kick off a four-day, three-game run. After my performance during today's morning skate, I felt there was a good chance I wouldn't be playing tonight. I'd been home less than twenty-four hours and worrying where I stood with Kami was messing with me. My mother had called and told me about Kami's visit, which renewed my hopes. But I was still on edge. I wanted to take action.

I headed for the back of the plane so I could wallow alone. As I lifted my carry-on to put it into the overhead compartment, I was brought back to the moment just a few short days ago when the flight attendant made a comment about me being Ryleigh's dad.

My eyes stung, and I swiped a tear away. I had to get it together. I felt myself slipping into the old post-breakup Trask, and I hated myself for it. I also didn't understand it. Kami and I hadn't dated for three or four years. It'd hardly been a week. Why was I reacting this way? I stared out the window and wracked my brain to try to make sense of it.

"Can I sit here?"

I nodded at Coach Conway, and he dropped into the aisle seat. I braced myself for what I knew was coming.

"I'm going to start you tonight."

"What?" That made no sense. I'd been a disaster on the ice. "Why?"

"Because I recognize the funk you're in. And the only way out of it is to focus on something else. Like making sure we win tonight. Unless you think you need a few days off?"

"No, sir."

"Good. I called Kriz and Brewer. They're coming tonight."

"But—Alexei just had a baby. Why would he—"

"Because he's your friend, Emerson. You need an intervention to fix your mindset, and Dexter isn't here." Jason was traveling with the Denver Edge this week since their starting goalie had a family emergency.

"Yes, Coach."

MY MOOD CONTINUED TO SOUR THROUGH WARM-UPS, BUT I was playing better, so Coach went ahead and started me. It was a rough game. The Missoula Glaciers were an old team, but they'd just affiliated with the new NHL expansion team, and every player was looking to prove himself in the hopes of getting called up to the next level.

By the third period, I'd had enough of their violence, and when Noel got slammed into the boards by three of their guys at the same time, it looked like a coordinated attack. Our rookie had been unstoppable all night and had just scored his first hat trick for our team.

I joined the fray and threw off my gloves. The refs let us go at it until our backup came and it turned into an all-out brawl. I jumped on the right winger, who'd been roughing up Noel all night, and let out all of my frustration on his face.

His helmet came off, and we fell to the ice. I realized his eyes were closed and he wasn't fighting back. I hardly comprehended being pulled off of him and being ejected from the game. I stalked past our trainers and waved off their help. I didn't care that I had a cut on my face or if it was bleeding.

Back in the locker room, I stripped off my gear, throwing it at the cubby. I couldn't believe I'd knocked a guy out. It was true what they said—hurt people hurt people. I didn't want to be that person, though.

"I see Tiger is appropriate nickname, no? Never saw his claws come out quite like that." Alexei's broken English interrupted my internal pity party.

"What's causing this, Trask?" Kingston asked. I sat on the bench and pressed my lips together before I could say something I'd regret to my former teammates. Kingston sat beside me, and Alexei flanked me on the other side.

I filled them in on everything that had happened in the last few days. "I just can't seem to move on. Why can't I move on?"

"Maybe you're not meant to," Kingston said. "Maybe this is the one you fight for. It's only been a couple days, right? Are you even sure it's a breakup?"

"Important question." Alexei leaned in. "Are you thinking about future together with her, or can you not see past the present?"

That was easy. "Dude, if she asked me to quit hockey and

move back to South Carolina with her in May, I'd do it in a heartbeat."

Alexei clapped his hand hard on my back. "Then there is your answer. You must fight."

You must fight. Alexei's three simple words made everything incredibly clear. By the time we touched back down in Colorado Springs three days later, I had a plan.

30

KAMI

"Still no calls or texts?" Khloe joined me by my bedroom window as I watched Ryleigh play in the backyard with my dad.

I shook my head. On the bed behind me were our packed suitcases. Sutton had been released from the hospital yesterday, and Ryleigh has spent enough time with him over the past two days that he didn't fight me on my refusal to stay through the weekend. I needed to get back to work.

"You could go to that New Year's party. See what happens." She twirled a lock of her hair and shot me an innocent look. "You know Trask will be there."

"I don't know, Klo. I feel miserable without him, but I'm scared."

"Scared of what exactly? Being loved by a great guy who adores you and your daughter?"

"No ... I don't know. What if he turns out to be someone different from who he is now?" I hadn't been the best judge of character with Sutton. How could I set myself up for that again? Especially now that I had Ryleigh to think about.

"News flash: Trask is nothing like Sutton. I could tell that the second I met him. And you know the important things. And it's not like knowing someone for years worked in your favor the last time. What I'm saying is, not knowing the future is okay. But don't deny yourself the present because you're scared of history repeating itself. You're smart enough not to jump into anything that doesn't feel right. Do your feelings for Trask feel right?"

I nodded. "More right than I ever felt with Sutton." I sniffed. "I think that's why I'm such a mess. He has the power to hurt me worse than Sutton did."

"Then why are we even having this conversation? It sounds to me like your heart has already made up its mind. Tell the brain to back off, and go get that man already!"

I WAS BACK AT WORK THE NEXT MORNING, WORKING THE EARLY shift. Ryleigh was having a playdate with Natasha, and Kira offered to dress her and bring her to the party. The restaurant was surprisingly dead, and by noon Brenna and I had hung all the New Year's Eve decorations, refilled all the condiment containers, and prepped all the produce for dinner.

"You sure we aren't needed here tonight?" I asked. "I have a feeling it's going to be packed."

"It always is, and believe me when I say you don't want to be here." She straightened the last barstool and beckoned me to follow her.

I followed her to the office in the back. Her oldest brother, Keegan, sat at the desk typing steadily and looking at his computer screen with concern. In contrast, Drew leaned on the back of his chair and grinned at the screen.

"Uh-oh," Brenna said. "What is it?"

"We're just shy of two grand to beat last year's total revenue," Drew said excitedly. "Barring a total disaster. I'm so going to win this bet."

"I really didn't think we'd do it," the serious, studious Keegan muttered. He didn't come out front often, preferring to help his parents manage the business side of things.

"That's cause you're a pessimist." Drew tapped his shoulder and grinned at us. "And just because you didn't like the peanut butter brew, you thought everyone would hate it. What's up, Bren?"

"I wanted to let you know everything is prepped for tonight and to remind you Kami and I are out of here at three o'clock. Anything else you need us to do while it's slow out there?"

He shook his head. "Nope. I got the bar stocked, too. Gonna be a big night!"

The New Year's party at Coach Conway's house was in full swing when Brenna and I arrived just after six. Gemma Allaire, Noel's mother, answered the door and led us to a spare bedroom where the kids were playing. Ryleigh ran to give me a hug and then told me I could go. Brenna laughed and dragged me out of the room.

We ended up in the dining room with Kira and a few of the older Wags. I nodded and smiled enough to participate, but my senses were on full alert for Trask. Someone said he was outside with a group of players, so I was keeping an eye on the back door.

"Here they come," Brenna whispered in my ear. Trask, Jason, Brendan, and Rury came inside in a whoosh of cold air.

I stood up and rubbed my hands on my thighs. I looked at Brenna for support. She nodded, and I walked toward the guys, who were now leaning against the kitchen counter discussing their predictions for tonight's Denver Edge game. Trask saw me approach and excused himself from the group.

"Hey," I said. "It's good to see you. Thanks again for the invitation. Ryleigh is having a wonderful time."

His soulful eyes bored into mine. There was pain there, and I was pretty sure I'd caused it. "I'm glad you came."

An awkward silence screamed between us. I spoke quickly to fill it. "I'm sorry about last week. I—I think I'm ready to try again. I just—I'm not sure about—It's scary to—"

"Kami." Trask wrapped his fingers around mine and lifted our hands to his chest. "I don't want you to be scared of me or to have any regrets. I can't do this if you're not one hundred percent sure this is what you want."

My hands started to shake, and he let them go. I shook my head sadly. "I think a hundred percent might be more than I can give right now."

I practically ran away from him and back to the dining room. I needed to think, and I couldn't do it here. "Bren, can you keep an eye on Ryleigh for a bit? I need to run home."

"Did you forget something?"

"No. Yes. I—I just need some time and space. I won't be too long. Promise."

"Okay."

I grabbed my coat and purse and hustled through the chilly night to my car. I started it up and blasted the heat.

I let my head fall to the steering wheel. Its icy surface seemed to bring me clarity. What was I doing? I wasn't a runner. I wanted this.

I loved him.

I opened my purse and pulled out the small bubble envelope. As I fastened the delicate bracelet onto my wrist, a wave of hope rushed through me.

No more indecision. I was going for this. All of it.

31

TRASK

*A*fter Kami left, I found a seat on the couch to watch the game. I needed a distraction. The Edge's starting goaltender was having a bad night. It was his first game back after the undisclosed family emergency, and halfway through the second period, they sent in the backup goalie.

"Mr. Tiggerman?"

"Hey, sweet girl." I grinned at Ryleigh, and she climbed up onto my lap, clutching the toy puppy I'd given her. "Happy New Year."

"Happy New Year." She giggled. "Are you going to kiss my mommy at midnight?"

I smiled sadly. "I don't know. I was thinking about kissing Luna." I leaned in conspiratorially. "I heard she gives the biggest kisses."

That set Ryleigh off in a fit of giggles. Luna was Coach Conway's Great Pyrenees dog.

Next to us, Brendan gasped. "Oh, damn!"

I followed his gaze to the screen as everyone in the room reacted to a save gone wrong.

"Holy …!"

"Oh my God! So much blood!"

My stomach dropped. A pile-up in the crease led to the goaltender's glove flying off, and a skate blade found its way to his wrist. Blood spurted as whistles blew and players dispersed to make way for the doctor and trainers. None of us could pull our eyes from the screen.

"He's hurted!"

Snapping back to reality, I shielded Ryleigh's eyes from the gruesome replay and stood up, calling for Brenna.

This was bad. I looked over at Jason. His face had gone ghostly white. Lauren was whispering in his ear. One thing I'd learned from living with him was that being sliced by a skate blade was his biggest fear.

And this could have been him.

I handed Ryleigh to Brenna, who whisked her out of the room as Coach paused the game and stood in front of the TV. "I just got a text from one of my contacts inside the Edge organization that Slocum Bryant's hand was bent at an odd angle. I'm not going to speculate what that means except that Dexter will probably be leaving us for the rest of the season." He nodded at Jason. "Life can change in a second, boys. We know that, but if you haven't experienced it, it's just a cliché. Treasure every moment that you have, especially with the people you care about."

He went on, but my brain was stuck on that last line. I got up from the couch and slipped into a spare bedroom to call Alexei, who had texted a few times. He'd been Jason's roommate before me and wanted to know why he wasn't texting back.

The call went to voice mail. I sat on the bed, contemplating what to do next, when my phone signaled a video call from his wife, Ginny.

"Hey, Trask. Sorry Alexei missed your call." She flipped the screen. "Mari needed calming, and sometimes his shoulder is the only thing that works. I swear it's because he's so hot all the time. His internal temp, not—well, you know what I mean."

I smiled as she brought her phone closer to Alexei and their baby. Sure enough, she was passed out on his shoulder. "She's beautiful. Congratulations again."

"Thank you," Ginny said. "So, how's Jason?"

"White as a sheet. He's not really talking."

Alexei motioned for the phone and Ginny passed it to him. "Tell him I'll call him tomorrow."

"I will."

We chatted for a few more minutes, and it became clear to me that I wanted what Alexei and Ginny had. Not someday in the future but now. With Kami. With only Kami.

I'd never had such a strong feeling about anything or anyone. I'd take all she could give, even if it was just a little at first. I needed to find her.

I opened the door, and there she was. Red-rimmed eyes, makeup streaked.

She'd never looked so beautiful.

I held my arms open, and she lunged at me, wrapping her arms tightly around my chest and pushing me back into the room. Behind her, in the lit hallway, Brenna raised a finger to her lips and gently closed the door.

32

KAMI

I pushed Trask into the room and hugged him with everything I had. His arms closed around me as he moved backward to sit on the bed.

I stood and just looked at him. This beautiful, talented, caring soul wanted me, and I had been ready to throw it all away because I was afraid.

How stupid I was.

The time in my car was all I'd needed to say goodbye to my lingering fears. I wanted to be his, all in, wherever life took us.

I still couldn't speak, so I reached out to cup Trask's face and leaned in to kiss him. Just a gentle touch to lips. It was enough fuel to find my voice. "I'm sorry, Trask. I was wrong. I want to—can we—"

He cut me off with a kiss that brought me back to the Christmas tree in the park. How had that only been a few weeks ago? This kiss was even more. It felt like coming home. In a way, it was. It was a reunion after being apart, and once again I found myself comparing him with Sutton. For all the times he'd gone away, we'd never come together like this on his return. I'd never missed him as much as I'd missed Trask these last few days.

When I couldn't breathe anymore, I pulled back. "They say if you let a butterfly go and it comes back to you, it's yours to keep."

"I want you to keep me, Trask," I whispered. "I love you."

"I love you, too. More than I ever thought I could love anyone. We'll keep each other. I'll always fly home to you and *only* you. I promise."

"And Ryleigh?" I had to be certain. Her heart was fragile, too.

"And Ryleigh."

There was no stopping the tears—or my smile—at his words. We were both putting ourselves out there, at the risk of being hurt again, and it was okay. I believed with my heart and soul he cared about us deeply, and that was enough.

He pulled me onto his lap, and we just held each other for a few moments. Content didn't begin to describe the state of my mind in that moment.

"It's almost midnight," he whispered. "Coach is going to set off fireworks in the backyard. Let's go get Ryleigh?"

"Yes." I slipped my hand in his, and we made our way out back. Ryleigh was sitting on a blanket with Ava and Natasha. She ran up to us when she saw us.

"Dmitri says you have to kiss a boy at midnight!"

I laughed. "You don't have to, sweetie."

She looked at Trask and raised her arms. He picked her up, and she cupped his face. "I think you need to be kissed, Mr. Tiggerman."

His smile showed pure adoration. "I do. I plan to kiss your mommy at midnight."

"Yeah. But I'm going to kiss you first." He turned his head, and her lips connected with his cheek.

"Thanks, Ryleigh-girl. I did need that." He hugged her close, and when she wiggled, he let her down. Around us, guests began the countdown.

"Mommy! It's your turn!"

"Ten, nine, eight ..." Trask pulled me to him, and our noses touched.

"Happy New Year, Kami."

"Seven, six, five ..."

"Happy New Year, Trask."

"Four, three, two, one ..."

"Happy New Year!" Ryleigh yelled as Trask's lips came crashing down on mine. Fireworks lit the sky above us, but the biggest explosions were happening inside my heart.

I was all in, wherever this would take us.

I pulled my face back from his. "Trask?"

"Yeah?"

I slid my hands down to take his and lifted them so that they were pressed to my heart. "I ... I love you. I know it seems soon to say, that, but—"

"Kami." He lifted our joined hands higher and placed a gentle kiss on my knuckles. "I love you, too. I'm pretty sure I've loved you from the moment I saw you. I can't explain it, but I felt—"

"A connection." We spoke at the same time, and then we were kissing again.

"And I love you both!" Without a word, Trask and I bent to scoop Ryleigh into our arms.

A new year and a new beginning. I couldn't wait to see where the future would take us.

EPILOGUE: TRASK

June

"It's not much farther, Mama." She looked so fragile, but she was walking on her own, mostly, aided only by a cane. Up until a month ago, she'd needed a walker. My dad was on her other side as we strolled into the garden at the Ellis's bee farm.

It was great to be home in South Carolina for the rest of the summer. The Voltage had made it to the playoffs, but we lost in the final round. I'd been called up to the Edge's roster to play a couple games for their playoff run, and then we'd stayed in Palmer City for the Brewer-Ranford weddings. Kami's sisters wanted to throw her a belated graduation party to celebrate her receiving her doctorate, and if all went to plan tonight, we'd be celebrating something else, too.

Yesterday, I'd brought over a dozen pots of milkweed to help Ryleigh create her own butterfly garden. As the cluster came into sight, her little curly-haired ponytail and big blue bow appeared over the tops of the plants as she stood up.

"Any butterflies yet?" I called.

Ryleigh looked up from the milkweed bush and bolted toward me. "Tiggerman!" I scooped her up, and she kissed my nose.

"How's my Ryleigh-girl?"

"I'm *so* good! We want to marry you!" She clapped her hands over her mouth. "Oh no! Mommy was supposed to say that!" She cast a worried glance over her shoulder to her mother, whose face was as red as Ryleigh's Princess Elana dress.

My heart stopped, then began racing. I grinned at Kami, then pressed my nose to Ryleigh's. "I promise I won't mention it, okay?"

"Okay!" She giggled. "I know! I'll try again. *I* say, 'Tiggerman, me and Mommy love you very much.' And *then* I give you BIG HUG!" She wrapped her little arms around my neck. I closed my eyes and held her tight, moved beyond measure that they wanted me to be a part of their lives forever.

"And then Mommy says—" She twisted around to face Kami, who looked panic-stricken. Behind her, her parents and sisters stood back from us, smiling like foxes in the henhouse. I had a feeling she hadn't meant to do this in front of everyone, but here we were.

Kami met my gaze and dropped to one knee. I grinned and shifted Ryleigh in my arms so I could reach into my pocket for the little box I'd brought with me. "Trask, I—I never thought I'd find love again. You surprised me, in every way. Every *good* way." She glanced around us and swallowed.

I held Ryleigh tight and sank to one knee, mirroring Kami's position and holding Ryleigh in place on my thigh.

"You surprised me, too," I said, pulling the box out of my pocket.

Kami gasped, and I flicked the box open.

"There's two rings in there, Mommy!" Ryleigh smacked her hands over my cheeks and turned my head to face her. "Is the little one for me? Or for Mommy's baby finger?"

I laughed and tried to talk as she squished my face. "It's for you, if you want it."

"I do!" She dropped her hands from my face and carefully pulled the little ring up from the cushion. "It's soooooo sparkly." She watched it twinkle in awe. "Okay! Put it on my finger now, please!"

I laughed and turned back to Kami. "I had a whole speech planned."

She smiled. "So did I."

"So did I!" Ryleigh shouted. She plucked the other ring from the box. "Mr. Tiggerman, will you marry us and love us for ever and ever and ever?"

I stared into Kami's eyes, barely noticing Khloe behind her, recording us with her phone. "I absolutely will."

"Good! Now take the rings and ask us to marry you! Me first."

"Yes, ma'am." She placed the smaller one in my waiting palm, and I held it up. "Ryleigh Emmaline Spencer, will you let me marry your mommy and be your stepdad?"

"I will!" She giggled as I slid the tiny ring onto her right-hand ring finger. "Now it's Mommy's turn!" She slid off my leg and ran to stand with her grandparents and aunts.

I stared at Kami, suddenly feeling shy. "I'm the luckiest guy in the world," I choked out. "It's hard to believe someone like you wants to love me forever."

"You're worthy of the best love, Trask. I'm overflowing with love for you."

I opened my mouth, but instead of words, I could only manage a whisper. My throat was thick with emotion, and I was trying not to cry in front of our families. "I love you more than anything, Kami. I'm already the happiest man in the world. Will you give me the honor of being your husband?"

She nodded. "It will be an honor to be your wife."

I slid the ring on her finger and pulled her close as clapping and whooping erupted around us. We stood up, and I kissed her like there'd be no tomorrow.

Thank you for reading *Christmas on Ice!*
Reviews are an author's best friend! Please leave a review at your favorite bookstore, Goodreads and BookBub.

Visit KerryEvelyn.com to join my newsletter and gain access to my Freebies page, which contains Bonus Content, including free stories, printables, and the full Palmer City Voltage Roster!

Want more Palmer City Voltage?
Check out the prequel, *Love on the Ice*,
and Book 1, *Cruising on Ice!*

And look for Coach Conway and Gemma's story, *Melting the Ice,* featured in the *Late to Love anthology,* releasing February 15, 2022! More than two dozen authors have come together to support our bookish friend who is battling cancer. All proceeds from the sale of the book go to #TeamPinkforTeri

Turn the page to meet Coach Conway and Noel's mom, Gemma, and read the first three chapters of their story!

Melting the Ice

Gemma

Brain freeze.

I winced and pressed the fingertips of my free hand into my forehead. The icy jolt of caffeine and sugar from the frozen coffee was having more than the desired effect.

My eyes were dry and gritty, since I'd hardly slept in two days. I wanted to make the drive from Toronto to Palmer City, Colorado, as quickly as possible. Less than an hour left to go, and if I didn't hit any traffic in Colorado Springs, I'd make it to the Plex, where my son Noel was practicing for his minor league hockey team, right at the end of his morning practice.

Three weeks had dragged by since I'd seen him last. He was eighteen, a recent high school graduate, and all by himself in a new city. He'd been drafted by Denver's professional team, the Edge, and sent down to their minor league team, the Palmer City Voltage, after training camp.

To be honest, I was glad about that. I didn't think Noel was ready to be an NHL star, in a foreign country, all by himself. For the thousandth time, I lifted a silent prayer of thanks that my boss allowed me to work remotely so I didn't have to report to the company's Toronto headquarters.

For the last couple of years, Noel and I had been super

transient following his hockey dreams. My best friend, Corey, was like a dad to Noel and helped when he could. We grew up next door to each other until my parents died, when I rented out our house and moved myself and Noel in with Corey and his family. His parents were the only grandparents Noel had ever known.

But Noel hadn't been drafted by the Toronto team or any Canadian team, for that matter. Though he'd have to cross the border to make his dreams come true, I was incredibly proud of him.

Corey had taught him everything he knew about the game and planned out Noel's path. I always wondered whether Corey would have pursued a hockey career himself if I hadn't gotten pregnant with Noel after a teenage party I barely remembered. Instead of leading a life of snipes and cellies, he helped me raise my son.

We were quite a pair, Corey and I. Like an old married couple, we joked. Not an ounce of attraction but plenty of mutual respect and admiration. Everyone always asked why we never just got married—to each other or anyone else, for that matter. If the well-wishers only knew how damaged the two of us were, they'd mind their own business. We kept each other's secrets, and there were agreements never to mention certain things. In this way, we thrived on the outside and survived on the inside.

I exited the highway and turned onto Main Street. A roadside marker explained that the adjacent Snowpack Creek divided the old mining town into east and west sides. Noel's coach, a former professional player named Zander Conway, had explained the older part of town was east of the creek. On the west side, newer developments built on old ranch property dotted the landscape from the creek to the mountains. To my right, the Rockies rose high and reminded me of the backdrops in old Western movies. They almost didn't look real.

A few turns later, I found the Plex and followed the signs to the ice rinks. *All right, Gemma. You have to stay awake just a little longer.* I parked the car and took a slow sip of my still-frozen coffee while I checked my phone for texts.

One message was from Corey, reminding me to text him when I arrived, and one from Noel, saying his phone would be in his locker during practice and to look for the Wags when I entered the rink. I felt uncomfortable about looking for the wives and girlfriends in the stands. I was his mom, and though I was only thirty-four, I was sure most of those women would be much younger.

I texted Corey—*Made it!*—and got out of the car. Ten minutes left of practice. I could watch from the floor at ice level. I didn't have it in me to make new friends right now. I'd find the Wags when I was well-rested and not feeling so out of sorts.

Zander

"Puck bunny in the hallway!"

"She's hot!"

"Who let her in?"

"She's not a puck bunny! That's my mom. Back off!"

"Oh. Sorry, dude."

Oh, hell. I pushed open the locker room door, and the sea of Voltage players parted. Noel Allaire, arms crossed and glaring at his new teammates, was trying to block them from getting any closer to his mother.

I hadn't met her in person yet, but we'd phoned and texted over the last couple of months since her son was drafted to Denver. He was a talented player but young, and they'd sent him to my team to get more experience before the Edge would consider adding them to their roster.

My gaze landed on the petite woman behind Noel. Gemma was even more stunning in person than what I'd seen on her social media. Understated but commanding. If she wore makeup, I couldn't tell. Her long brown waves, skinny jeans, and white bubble jacket gave her a youthful look, but I knew she was in her mid-thirties, just a few years younger than me.

I caught her eyes, effectively trapping my mouth shut.

I should say something.

"Ahem." The players swiveled their heads in my direction. Noel continued to glare. No doubt this wasn't the first time he'd dealt with this. Gemma looked like she could be his sister. "There will be extra laps and heavy fines, with possible removal from this organization, for anyone who disrespects Ms. Allaire or any other woman, a part of this organization or not. Am I understood?"

Shaking my head to the chorus of "Yes, Coach," I hoped what I'd overheard was the worst of it. My players were good guys, but most were under twenty-five, and their brains weren't fully developed yet. Add in the concussions, and sometimes, they didn't make the best decisions. I felt it was my duty to coach them not just in hockey, but in life. The world was a scary place, and most of these kids had lived in a hockey bubble. It had its pros and cons.

"Good." I nodded. "Now get out of here. Allaire, you stay."

Noel relaxed his shoulders, and his mother patted his arm. "Sorry, sweetie," she said. "I know you hate when that happens. I do, too."

He sighed. "It's fine. I'm proud of you, Mom. And you *are* pretty. It just makes me mad when guys remark on it."

I walked over to them and offered my hand. "Zander Conway." Gemma took it and smiled up at me. Her eyes were a dark blue, almost indigo, and so distracting I had to work to focus on what I was going to say. "It's great to finally meet you in person. I'm sorry that happened. They should know better."

"Call me Gemma. No worries. We're used to it." She flashed another grin, and it shot straight to my heart. Her effect on me caught me off guard, and I didn't like it. It wasn't right to feel attracted to a player's family member.

"Still, it's not cool. Are you free for lunch?" I asked. They exchanged a glance, and I groaned. *"Both* of you." What a gaffe, especially after getting on the players for thinking about picking her up. I must sound like a total chump.

"Mom? Didn't you text you've been up for two days straight?" Noel kept his gaze fixed on me.

Smart kid.

I cleared my throat and rubbed the back of my neck. "It's not a big deal. It's just, I thought … you know, since Noel's been staying with me, I could fill you in on some things."

Gemma pulled her lips into her mouth as she thought. She slowly released them, and as they filled back out, I fixated on the pink and pillowy skin forming into a cupid's bow.

Noel cleared his throat, and my eyes snapped up to meet hers.

Gemma smirked, but then she smiled. "Sure. I could definitely eat. And my room won't be ready until after two o'clock." She shook her head. "The extended stay place your back office recommended just texted me that they lost my reservation and needed more time. At this point, I need fuel to stay awake, and coffee by itself ain't cutting it."

"I'm really sorry to hear that." What a lame reply. Should I offer her my other guest room? Probably not a good idea.

Noel's eyes darted between Gemma and me, and I realized I was staring again.

"Well, let's go, then," I said. "Noel, your choice. Brewski's or Paddy Maroon's?"

"Neither." He adjusted his crossed arms. "Where's a place the team won't go?"

I smiled wryly. "There's a veggie wrap place just over the creek."

"Sounds perfect," he said. Gemma and I exchanged an amused glance as Noel turned toward the exit, adjusted the strap of the duffel bag on his shoulder, and held the door, waiting.

I followed them out to the parking lot and watched them get into a packed older model Highlander. Every window was obstructed by boxes, and there was a bin secured to the roof. Gemma had definitely come prepared to stay for a while.

My insides flip-flopped at the idea of seeing more of her.

Gemma

"Hi, Dad!"

"Hey, kiddo! Hey, Gem!"

"Hey, Cor. I see it's Cat Day again?" In a back corner booth at Brewski's Sports Bar and Grille—I'd made it clear to Noel that veggie wraps would not be enough sustenance after my trek—I held my phone between us while Noel face-timed Corey. My best friend's heavily made-up face stared back at us. Corey was a make-up artist specializing in prosthetics and taught classes several times a week. I was grateful he'd answered the call. Sometimes he got so caught up in his work, even between classes like right now, that he often didn't hear his phone ringing.

I handed the device over and took a long sip of my double espresso-infused coffee, closing my eyes as I breathed in the aroma, hoping it would help in my efforts to rival Energizer Bunny.

Corey had called Noel "Dad" since kindergarten. He'd come home from school one day and told us about the other kids having mommies and daddies. When he asked Corey if he could call him Daddy, we'd both cried at the request. I think that was probably one of the best moments of Corey's life.

A few years later, he asked why we didn't have any wedding pictures, and why our last names were different, and Corey and I had had some explaining to do. I knew our living arrangement was confusing, but it worked for us. Every family was different, and that's what we focused on. As long there was love and respect, and everyone was safe, we were good.

"My teammates picked a nickname for me today," Noel told Corey. I glanced across the table at Zander. He pressed his lips tight and winked.

I turned to Noel. "And?"

His cheeks filled with air and he let out a long, slow breath, a technique Corey had taught him when he was an emotional three-nager. It'd been the terrible three's for this kid, who'd still wanted to cuddle at two years old. Three had been another story, and hockey had helped channel a lot of those big feelings.

"Spill it," Corey encouraged. "It can't be that bad."

I stole another glance at Zander across the table. His face was beet-red. Whatever it was, I needed to be ready to empathize. He really *was* trying not to laugh. I stifled a giggle at the incredibly endearing expression on his face.

Noel sighed. "It's ... ugh ... seriously. It's so dumb!"

"Dude, you're eighteen and a rookie. *Of course* it's dumb. That's what makes it fun." Corey was always one hundred percent honest.

Noel's shoulders relaxed. Corey had always had a talent for diffusing Noel's frustration. "They're calling me Santa."

I covered my mouth with my hand when I met Zander's gaze again. He'd also covered his mouth, and I think I heard him snort.

Corey's laugh broke the ice for all of us. I let my giggle loose and Zander did his best to control his amusement. I couldn't help looking at the man. He had the easy confidence of an athlete, but was softer in a way I couldn't explain. His close-cropped jet-back hair and shadowy stubble along his jawline framed a face that could have been right out of *GQ* magazine.

"Ugh, Mom. You're not supposed to laugh," Noel was definitely annoyed with me. "I understand Dad laughing, but you're supposed to be on my side."

"I'm sorry! All right, let Coach fill us in with the parental stuff so Corey can get back to work." Noel's serious manner sometimes made it difficult to empathize. He sweated the small things, and sometimes our sense of humor didn't match up. Corey understood him a little better, having a sister with zero sense of humor, so I was glad for that.

Noel handed the phone back to me and I leaned it against the napkin dispenser so we could all see each other. Noel had told Zander about his non-traditional upbringing, so I didn't have to explain.

I sat back to listen as Zander summed up the last few weeks, reviewing the details pertinent for a Canadian citizen playing in the States, and answering questions from Corey about the schedule, goals for improvement, and the Colorado Springs area. He had a Michigander accent, and I wondered where he'd grown up. Likely not far from Toronto, and I made a mental note to ask him later.

Zander the Michigander. I tried not to giggle. Lord, I needed sleep.

I didn't know what to ask, so I was glad Corey had played up through college and had had a general idea of what we could expect. Noel had been offered scholarships to several universities, but he really wanted to try going pro first. We respected that, and were adamant he carve out the path he felt led to follow. It sounded like he'd be in Palmer City for at least half the season, so we'd have to get an apartment.

My phone buzzed and a text flashed across the top of the screen. I caught *"We're sorry …"* before it disappeared.

"Crap!" It had to be the hotel.

"What is it?" Corey asked.

"Hold on a sec." I picked up the phone and opened the text app.

We're sorry to inform you your reservation has been canceled. Please return our call if we can be of further assistance in helping you locate a suitable accommodation.

I closed my eyes and mentally counted to ten. What was I supposed to do now? I was so tired I was ready to sleep in my car.

"Gem? I'm still looking at your chin. You okay?" Corey's concern jogged me from my counting.

"Who's it from, Mom?"

"Sorry." I swiped out of the app and adjusted the phone. "That was my hotel. They canceled my reservation." I blinked back tears as I processed what this meant. "I...I just really need to sleep right now." My voice went up in pitch with each word.

I couldn't break down in front of my son and his coach. "Noel, can you use your phone to video call your dad? You all can catch me up later. I'm going to go to my car and try to find another place to stay."

"No need." I jerked my head to Zander. He tapped his fingertips on the table and smiled shyly. "I have an extra guest room. You and Noel are welcome to stay as long as you want."

Zander

It was the gentlemanly thing to do. The poor woman was showing signs of exhaustion.

"Are you sure you don't mind? I feel like I'm about to crash. Just for tonight. And then I can—" Gemma's pitch increased with each word. I wanted to help more than I wanted to win our next game, but I had to play it cool.

"It's fine, really. And the house next door is a monthly rental. It's empty right now. If you'd like, I can check with their management company and see if it's available."

"That would be amazing. If it's in our budget ... What do you think, Noel?" She pulled her hair over her left shoulder and looked up at her son, who was still frowning.

His eyes narrowed, and rightly so. But he had nothing to worry about. I wouldn't pursue his mother. But I could help with the lodging issue, so I would.

"I guess." His expression softened. "Mom, let me drive, though. You're tired, and I know the way."

Yeah, he was a great kid. I signaled for the check and held up my hand when Gemma pulled out her wallet. "I got this."

"Let me tip then." I had the sense not to argue with her, and ten minutes later I was in my car, driving home, and thinking about how glad I was I'd hired that cleaning service when Noel moved in.

While Gemma napped, Noel and I unloaded her SUV. Later that night, I was watching footage in my office when I heard a knock at the door. Luna, my Great Pyrenees dog, lifted her head.

"Easy, girl," I whispered, scratching her on the head. "Come in!" I swung my chair around to find Gemma in the doorway. The combination of her hair piled on top of her head in a wild bun and her tired eyes stirred a desire for her, but it wasn't simply attraction. An unfamiliar, protective instinct was screaming inside me to connect with her on a deeper level.

"I wanted to thank you for letting us stay here," she said. "You mentioned the house next door?"

Right. I scribbled the management company's name on my notepad and tore off the sheet. "Ask for Devin. He's the property manager, and mention that you're staying here." I handed it to her. "With any luck, we'll be able to move you in tomorrow night."

"That's amazing. Thank you." Our fingers brushed in the exchange, and our eyes connected. Neither of us spoke.

I'm not sure how long we stared. Her gaze drifted to Luna as the dog stood up and stretched, her loud yawn filling the silence. The trill of Gemma's phone broke the spell, and she jumped. I cleared my throat as she pulled the phone from her pocket. "It's Corey. Thanks again, Zander."

"You're welcome." I exhaled slowly and watched her go, followed by Luna. *Traitor.* How did I become bewitched so quickly? There was no doubt in my mind I was under Gemma's spell. As I sat there, the irony didn't escape me that after so many years alone, I finally felt something for someone. But unfortunately for me, my potential new next-door neighbor was someone that I couldn't ever have.

Don't miss *Melting the Ice*, which will be featured in a limited-run charity anthology, *Late to Love*, which will be available February 15-July 31, 2022.

ACKNOWLEDGMENTS

Special thanks to Andrew Kuligowski and Mike Valcy, who I'm sure groan at this point every time they see a message from me pop up in their notifications! I'm so grateful to the two of you. Without your knowledge of the game and your kind, sharing hearts, these hockey stories wouldn't be what they are.

To Layla and Verity, whose bright smiles and Tuesday morning check-ins encouraged me to keep writing, even when my creative was drained. You girls rock! 😊

This book would never have been finished without the help of my crit partners, beta readers, and editors! Thanks for being there for me, especially when my creativity was drained. In ABC order, because there is no fair way to list you: Angelique, Brenna, Candace, Chelsea, Chris, Jill, Judy, Korin, Lauren, Laurie, Lila, Megan, Pam, Sarah, Stephanie, Tammy, TJ, Tonya, and those who wish to remain anonymous!

To my ARC readers, I am so looking forward to your reviews on this one! Thank you for dedicating several hours of your life to my words and sharing with the world what you think about them in your reviews!

To the Crane's Cove Crew members, thanks for helping me build up Palmer City and making suggestions for small-town must-haves! More are coming, and a map, too! Stay tuned...

As always, thanks to my family and the Big Guy above for making this all possible! MWAAH!

ABOUT THE AUTHOR

Kerry Evelyn is the author of the Crane's Cove series, #sweetresortromance set in Coastal Maine, the Palmer City Voltage #sweethockeyromance series, and several short stories that span multiple genres. She's also a Guest Author for the Cat's Paw Cove romance series, a writing instructor, and a contest judge. A native of the Massachusetts SouthCoast, Kerry changed her latitude in 2002 and now calls the Orlando area home. Fueled on faith, Dunkin' iced coffee, and a love for people, including her amazing family, Kerry loves (in ever-changing order) books, boy bands, cats, hockey, sweet drinks, taking selfies, traveling, and the madness of getting the stories in her head onto the page.

Website: KerryEvelyn.com/links
Reader Group: Facebook.com/groups/CranesCoveCrew

facebook.com/KerryEvelynAuthor
amazon.com/Kerry-Evelyn/e/B077LWTYXJ
instagram.com/KerryEvelynAuthor
twitter.com/theKerryEvelyn
bookbub.com/authors/kerry-evelyn

Also by Kerry Evelyn

Crane's Cove

Love on the Edge

Love on the Rocks

Love on the Beach

Love on the Fly

A Night at the Inn: A Lizzie Borden Short Story

The Cotton Candy Caper: A Fall Carnival Story

A Night in the Passage: A Crane's Cove Short Story

The Fisherman Nutcracker: A Whimsical Christmas Story

A Night in the Cabin: A Crane's Cove Short Story

A Second Shot at Love: A Second Chance Romance Novelette

A Home for Christmas: A Sweet Southern Christmas Story

Cat's Paw Cove

Moon Mist Manor Book 1: Christmas at Moon Mist Manor

Moon Mist Manor Book 2: Love Overrules the Lawyer

Moon Mist Manor Book 3 The Beachcomber's Buccaneer Bounty

Palmer City Voltage

Love on the Ice: A Hockey Romance Novelette

Cruising on Ice: A Sweet Friends-to Lovers Hockey Romance

Christmas on Ice: A Sweet Holiday Hockey Romance

Sparks on the Ice (Subscriber Bonus)

Melting the Ice: A Sweet Late to Love Romance (Late to Love Anthology)

Celebration on Ice: A Sweet Second-Chance Romance

Crushing on Ice: A Sweet Wedding Romance

Once Upon Academy

Birds of a Feather (Prequel)

Bird's Eye View (Once Upon Academy Volume 1)

Phoenix Rising (A Once Upon Academy Duet)

Nonfiction

City Nights (How I Met My Other Anthology)

Fenway: A Beacon of Hope (How I Met My Other 2 Anthology)

The Believer's Journal for Everyday Faith

The Advent Experience Keepsake Planner

How to Binge-Write Your Novel